Too Many Deaths

By
James R. Coggins

Mill Lake Books

Published by Mill Lake Books
Chilliwack, BC
Canada
jamescoggins.wordpress.com/mill-lake-books

Printed by Lightning Source, distributed by Ingram

ISBN: 978-1-998787-04-3

For Jaeda
and her family

Other books by James R. Coggins

John Smyth Mysteries
Who's Grace?
Desolation Highway
Mountaintop Drive
Springtime in Winnipeg

Other Fiction
1995: Je me souviens

Nonfiction
John Smyth's Congregation: English Separatism, Mennonite Influence and the Elect Nation
Living for God in a Pagan Society: What Daniel Can Teach Us

Table of Contents

Too Many Deaths

"There have been too many deaths."

"Yeah, Sergeant." Constable Edwards sighed. "I'm tired of coming to accident scenes myself. It's always the same things—speed, alcohol, and carelessness. No matter how many education programs we run, people keep doing the same things."

"That's not what I meant."

"What?"

"Never mind. Tell me about this accident."

"It's pretty clear." Edwards pointed. "The SUV came too fast around that curve and slid sideways—you can see how it ploughed up the gravel at the edge of the road. The rear wheels slid off the road there, and it flipped over. Looks like it rolled several times before hitting the tree."

Sergeant Wesson looked down the embankment about a hundred meters to where the crumpled vehicle lay on its side against a large evergreen. Another officer and two paramedics were strapping a white bundle onto a gurney.

"The paramedics think she probably died instantly," Edwards said.

Wesson shrugged. "Any idea when it happened?"

"Sometime last night. Engine's cold. Rigor is setting in. Unless somebody saw it happen, nobody would see the SUV way down there until morning."

"It's visible enough now."

"Sure. Directly in the line of vision as cars come down the hill and around the bend. The driver who reported it saw it right away."

"I suppose that driver has an alibi for the time of the accident?"

"Oh, yeah. I checked."

"Any other vehicles involved?"

"Doesn't look like it. There are no other skid marks."

"It's a gravel road. I suppose other traffic might have shifted the gravel and covered them up," Wesson mused.

"It's possible, but there's not a lot of traffic on this road."

"Well, make sure. Check for foreign paint on the SUV."

"We always do," Edwards said.

"Do you have an ID?"

"Not yet. The way the car is lying, we had to get the body out before we could look for an ID or search the vehicle for any other evidence. I ran the plates, and the SUV is registered to a Moose Mountain Lodge."

Wesson nodded. "Come and report to me when you have processed the scene."

"Sure, I'll do that," Edwards said. "What are you doing here anyway? You don't usually come to accident scenes."

"I already told you," Wesson answered. "There have been too many deaths."

*****

It was almost noon when Edwards walked into Wesson's office.

"Finished processing the scene?" Wesson asked.

"Yeah, the SUV is in the yard, and the techs are still going over it."

"Do you have a name?"

"There was a purse. Her ID says she is Lisa Thornton, aged thirty-eight. She apparently lives at Moose Mountain Lodge. I checked that out too. There's a website. It's a hunting and fishing lodge about an hour farther up the gravel road she was on."

"Does anything about the name of the lodge strike you?"

Edwards paused, indicating he had not been expecting this question. "Not really."

"Never mind. We can discuss it later. Anything else?"

"One odd thing. There was a loaded hunting rifle in the front seat of the SUV."

Wesson sat up straighter. "What make and model?"

Edwards consulted his notes. "A Remington 7600."

"Are you sure it was originally in the front seat? Could it have been in the back and flown forward in the accident?"

Edwards considered this. "Things happen, but I don't think so. The butt was pushed down between the two front seats. It looked like it had been deliberately put there so it would be within easy reach."

When Wesson didn't say anything, Edwards continued. "I don't know about any family, and we need someone to positively identify the body. I phoned the lodge several times, but there was no answer. I'm going to drive up there now."

Wesson started to say something, then stopped. "Go ahead. Let me know what you find. And if you can get access, check the phone up there for recent calls. Make a record of each one."

Edwards shrugged. "Sure. Anything else?"

Wesson looked hard at the younger officer. "You haven't considered the key question."

When he said nothing further, Edwards asked, "What's that?"

"Why was Lisa Thornton driving down that road late at night with a loaded hunting rifle?"

Edwards scratched the side of his face. "Don't know. Maybe she was sick. Maybe she was driving into town to buy something. Or maybe she was bringing the rifle down to be repaired."

"A one-hour drive each way late at night?" Wesson asked.

Edwards shrugged. "Maybe she wasn't thinking clearly. Or maybe I'll find out something when I go up to the lodge."

"A first principle of police work—and a lot more," Wesson said. "If you want to understand what is happening in the present, you have to know what happened in the past."

Edwards was used to the sergeant's habit of offering proverbial advice and just shrugged.

*****

It was late in the day, but, when Edwards returned, Wesson was waiting for him and called him into his office. "What did you find?" he asked.

Edwards sat in the chair opposite Wesson's desk. "Moose Mountain Lodge is an impressive place," he began. "It's in a big clearing up in the mountains near the end of that road. There's a two-story log building a couple of hundred feet long. There didn't appear to be anyone there. I looked around the clearing and even called out. Then I went up onto the porch. Big double doors, locked. I had the dead woman's keys, and I was trying the different keys in the lock when I sensed something wasn't right. I looked back, and there was this Indian standing two feet behind me. Snuck right up on me. I never heard a thing. I could have shot him."

"Or he could have shot you."

Edwards shrugged. "Anyway, this Indian—"

"First Nations man."

"What?"

"First Nations man or Native or Indigenous," Wesson repeated. "He probably wasn't from India."

"No, he was Native," Edwards said. "Older guy, in his fifties or sixties. Not very tall, maybe five eight, and overweight. He said his name was George Tessam. He and his wife Mary are caretakers at the place. There's the main lodge building and then some smaller log cabins scattered in the trees behind it and to one side. They live in the one farthest away from the main building."

"What did he tell you about Lisa Thornton?"

"He said she owns the lodge, and she lived in the main building."

"Anybody else there? Hunters?" Wesson asked.

"No, Tessam said there were no guests. It's not hunting season."

"Did you see any moose?"

"No. No moose."

"Of course not. You don't find moose up at the top of mountains. They prefer swamps and beaver ponds down in the valleys." Wesson smiled. "But the name sounds good—

Moose Mountain Lodge. Attracts the American hunters who don't know any better. Did you know that there are seven Moose Mountains in the US? Three of them are in New York State."

"Uh, no, I didn't know that." After a moment, Edwards shrugged and continued. "I showed him the picture of the dead woman, and he said it was Lisa Thornton. He said he had heard her drive out about 10:30 last night, but she hadn't said anything to him, so he didn't know where she was going."

"Did you ask him about the gun?"

"Yeah, he said he thought it was hers, the one she uses for target practice and occasionally takes on hunts, but he didn't know why she would have it with her in the SUV."

"Did he say anything else?"

"No. He wasn't very talkative. He answered my questions but didn't volunteer anything. Typical Indian."

"You mean typical...never mind," Wesson said. "What did you do next?"

"I told him I was going to look through the lodge. He told me a bit about the layout, but then left me to it."

"An impressive place, you said?"

"Yeah. You go in through the main double doors and you're in this big lobby, two stories, right up to the rafters. The registration desk is straight ahead, with big stone fireplaces on both sides. There is a stairs at each end of the lobby, which leads up to the second floor. The wing on the left is just motel-type rooms on both floors, on both sides of a central hallway. The right wing is the same upstairs, but the bottom floor is a dining hall and kitchen. Behind the reception desk is a big office, and to the right of that is a locked equipment room full of hunting rifles and fishing equipment. There is a stairs in the office that leads up to the owner's living quarters. There are a living room, a small kitchen, and a couple of bedrooms, one of them apparently in use, hers. Oh, yeah, and there was a door cut in the office wall to the left, connecting it to the first guest room on the bottom floor."

"Did you look through the office?"

"Oh, yeah. Pretty much what you'd expect—bills, business records, that sort of thing. There was a business card on the desk for a lawyer, guy named Lloyd Simmons. He's got an office here in town."

"Did you check the phone?"

"Yeah. I made a list. There was call display. There were a couple of messages from hunters from the States, wanting to make reservations. There were a couple of calls at different times from callers whose identity was blocked, maybe telemarketers. There was a call a few days ago from this lawyer." Edwards paused. "The most interesting one was from a number that looked like it was for a cell phone. The caller's name was John Seymour. It came in at 10:13 the night she died."

"John Seymour? Very interesting," Wesson said. "You think that phone call might be what made her come driving down the mountain in the dark?"

"Could be."

"Did you try calling the number?"

"Yeah, but it's turned off. Went straight to voice mail."

"Anything else of significance?"

"One thing. There were a lot of empty liquor bottles, mostly whiskey, in the office and in the bedroom that appeared to be in use."

"That raises the question of whether she might have been drinking and driving."

"Yeah. I guess the autopsy will tell us."

"We still need someone to positively identify the body. Did you ask the caretaker to come down?"

"Yeah, afterward I went and found him again. He didn't want to come down and look at the body, maybe some Indian superstition about being afraid of dead bodies or something. He said that there's no other family up there. He said her mother used to live up there with her, but she died a couple of weeks ago. I figured I would go and see this lawyer. If he's the family lawyer, maybe he could identify her."

"Good idea." Wesson thought for a moment. "Let's go together."

Lloyd Simmons's office was on the second floor of a century-old office building above a bank. The building was classical but dated, elegant but no longer fashionable. When they explained their purpose to a twenty-something receptionist, she directed them to a small waiting area with a black leather couch and two chairs. About ten minutes later, she ushered them down a short hall. She knocked on a solid oak door, then led them through it. It was a large office about twenty feet square. Lloyd Simmons appeared to be a little over six feet tall but slightly stooped. He was wearing a traditional, dark blue, three-piece suit. He was clean-shaven, with a full head of hair that was silver rather than white. He stood when they entered, but did not offer to shake hands, instead gesturing toward two leather chairs in front of his large mahogany desk.

When they were seated, Simmons smiled politely and asked, "What can I do for you, officers?"

It had been agreed that the constable would take the lead in the questioning while Wesson observed. "I am Constable Edwards, and this is Sergeant Wesson. We understand that you represent a woman named Lisa Thornton?"

"Lisa Thornton is a client of mine, yes," the lawyer said, "but I am afraid I can't discuss any of the legal matters I handle for her."

"We understand that," the constable said. "We understand lawyer-client privilege. However, we believe Lisa Thornton was killed in a vehicle accident yesterday."

"Oh, dear," the lawyer replied. After a moment, he added, "But what do you mean you believe she was killed? Don't you know?"

"We believe the person killed in the accident was Lisa Thornton, but the body has not yet been formally identified," Edwards answered. "Do you know of a family member who could make the identification?"

"No, there was just Lisa and her parents, who are both deceased. I don't believe there were any other close relatives. There are possibly some distant cousins, but I don't know of any and certainly none living here."

"Would you be willing and able to identify the body?" Edwards asked.

The older man was silent for a moment. "Yes, I could do that," he said.

*****

Fifteen minutes later, they were in the basement of the hospital outside the morgue. The lawyer had insisted on driving his own vehicle, an older model BMW.

"Are you ready for this?" Edwards asked.

The silver head nodded.

After they had entered and an attendant had pulled open a drawer and lowered a white sheet to reveal the face, the lawyer stared at the battered face of the dead woman. His expression never changed.

"Yes, I believe that is Lisa Thornton," he said.

"You are sure?" Edwards asked.

"The face is somewhat swollen, of course, but yes, I am sure," the lawyer said.

When they had gone back out into the hall, Wesson spoke for the first time. "Mr. Simmons, could you now tell us some things about Lisa Thornton? I think it would be best to do that either back at your office or at the police station."

"Let's go back to my office," Simmons said.

*****

When they had reconvened in the lawyer's office, Edwards took up the questioning again. "What can you tell us about Lisa Thornton?" he asked.

"It is not very complicated," Simmons said. "Lisa Thornton and her family have owned and operated the

16

Moose Mountain Lodge, which is a hunting and fishing lodge catering largely to Americans, for several decades."

"But her parents are deceased?" Edwards asked.

"Yes. Her mother died a couple of weeks ago, and her father a few weeks before that."

Edwards glanced over at Wesson, whose passive face revealed nothing. "That seems a bit odd, them all dying so close together. Were the deaths connected?"

"Not directly," Simmons said. "Lisa's father, John Seymour, died of a heart attack. He had had a history of heart problems and had had one previous attack. Lisa's mother, Annemarie..." The lawyer paused. "I believe the conclusion is that she committed suicide, possibly due to grief over the death of her husband. They were very close, a devoted couple."

"Why did you call Lisa a few days ago?" Wesson asked.

The lawyer did not seem disturbed by the sudden change of direction. "I called her to talk to her about her mother's estate."

"Are you the executor?" Wesson asked.

"No, Lisa was the executor. I was the secondary executor if Lisa wasn't able to serve as executor or if she was unwilling."

"Was she unable or unwilling?" Wesson continued.

"No, that wasn't an issue."

"So, what does the will say?" Wesson asked.

"It was relatively straightforward," the lawyer said. "The lodge was jointly owned by John and Annemarie. When he died, John's will left everything to Annemarie, but that provision is void since Annemarie did not survive him by thirty days. It doesn't really make any difference because John's will states that everything would go to Lisa if Annemarie also died, and Annemarie's will said the same thing."

"So, everything went to Lisa," Edwards said.

"Yes," the lawyer answered.

"But if Lisa is dead, who inherits the estate now?" Edwards asked.

"That is what I wanted to talk to Lisa about." The lawyer smiled in Wesson's direction. "Lisa did not have a will, and I was encouraging her to have one done."

"But she didn't do it?" Edwards asked.

"No."

"So, who does the estate go to?"

"As I said, as far as I know, there were only Lisa and her parents. Unless some relative comes forward that I don't know about, the estate will revert to the crown."

"Does that make you the executor of the estate?" Edwards asked.

"No, a public trustee will have to be appointed by the courts."

"Why didn't Lisa want to make a will?" Edwards asked.

The lawyer paused. "I am not entirely sure. Lisa Thornton wasn't overly fond of lawyers and the legal system, but, like a lot of younger adults, she didn't expect to die in the near future, so I suppose she was just putting it off until later. And, of course, she had recently lost both of her parents and already had a lot to deal with."

At this point, Wesson entered the conversation again. "Lisa Thornton has a different last name than her parents. Is she married, or was she married?"

"Was," the lawyer answered. "She was briefly married to an American, whom she met when he came to the lodge on a hunting trip. But he died only two or three years later. That was about fifteen years ago. They had no children."

Wesson stood. "Thank you for your assistance, Mr. Simmons," he said. "We will notify the public trustee's office about the situation. We'll get back to you if we have any further questions."

Tuesday, May 29

It was just after noon the next day when Edwards handed his preliminary report to Sergeant Wesson.

"I'll read it later," Wesson said. "Give me the short version."

Edwards was used to his sergeant's curt manner. He was ready with his answer. "It was pretty much what I expected. There were no foreign paint chips on the SUV, no other skid marks, and no evidence of another vehicle involved in the accident."

"Mechanical issues?"

"The techs are still examining the wreck, but nothing obvious. The brakes and steering appear to have been working. A couple of the tires are deflated, but the techs think that occurred in the roll down the hill. There is no evidence a tire blew out up on the road, no bits of rubber."

"What else?"

"The medical examiner says the woman died on impact or very shortly after. She had a blood alcohol level of point fourteen, close to twice the legal limit."

"Do you have a time of death?"

"The medical examiner estimated the time between ten o'clock and a little after midnight. The woman had a broken watch that said 11:23."

"So, it seems pretty straightforward?" Wesson said. "A routine traffic accident due to speed and alcohol."

"Yeah, I guess," Edwards said. When Wesson didn't say anything, he continued, "What do you want me to do next? It's odd that Lisa Thornton and her parents all died so close together. Do you want me to look into the deaths of her parents to see if there is anything suspicious there?"

Wesson did not reply. Instead, he picked up a folder from the corner of his desk and handed it to Edwards.

Edwards took it, opened it, sat down in a chair across from Wesson, and began reading. After a moment, he said, "This is the police report on her father's death, John Seymour. I thought he died of a heart attack?"

"He did, apparently," Wesson answered. "But it's a remote area, the family called 9-1-1 when they found the body, and the dispatcher thought that a police presence might be prudent, just to be sure."

Edwards continued reading. He suddenly sat up straight and looked at Wesson. "You wrote this report!" He made it sound like an accusation.

"That's right," Wesson answered.

"But I didn't know you went out on police calls. I thought you just..." he trailed off.

"You thought what?" Wesson asked. "That I just sat here in the office pushing paper?"

"No, I didn't mean that..."

"I occasionally go out in the field," Wesson said. "In this case, there was that big protest demonstration down at the port, we were shorthanded, and it was easier to just go myself rather than call someone in or pull someone out of the port detail."

"Okay, but it looks like it really was just a heart attack."

"Yes," Wesson said. "The autopsy report is there in the file. I thought it best to ask for an autopsy, just to be sure. The autopsy was very clear. John Seymour died of a heart attack."

"Was there anything suspicious that made you want an autopsy?"

"Not really," Wesson said. "Seymour died sometime in the night, the medical examiner thought maybe between two and three, but the family didn't find him until the morning."

"Why not?"

"Seymour had a bad heart. The family said his doctor told him to avoid strenuous exercise, including stairs, so he had begun sleeping in that suite on the ground floor that can be reached through the office. His wife and daughter continued to sleep in bedrooms on the second floor, above the office."

"So, Seymour died alone?"

"Yes, he was found on the floor beside the bed. It wasn't clear if he had gotten up to go to the bathroom or if he had felt the heart attack coming on and had gotten up to get his heart medication. We found that in the drawer of the bedside table. He had thrashed around a little bit on the floor, but there was nothing to suggest that anyone else had been there or this was anything more than what it seemed."

"But you ordered an autopsy anyway?"

Wesson shrugged. "I'm thorough. And since there were no witnesses, we didn't know for sure what he had died of. The family assumed heart attack simply because of his medical history." He paused a moment. "But the autopsy confirmed that he died of a heart attack, and I closed the case."

Edwards thought for a moment. "And I suppose the mother's death was also checked out thoroughly?"

Wesson reached over, picked up another file, and handed it to Edwards. Edwards began reading it, this time more carefully. When he was done, he looked up.

"You also wrote this report?" Edwards asked.

"Yes. Since I had been there before, Lisa Thornton called me directly when she found her mother, rather than calling 9-1-1."

"And it is clear that she committed suicide?"

"You read the report," Wesson answered. "She had taken an overdose of an antidepressant medication called Xanifol, washed down with wine. I called out a forensic team. Her fingerprints were on the wine bottle and the pill bottle, no one else's. The pills were hers, prescribed by her doctor. She even left a suicide note addressed to her daughter, saying, 'I'm sorry, Lisa. I'm going to join John.'"

"And it was her handwriting?"

"Yes. I had it confirmed by an expert."

"You don't have any doubts about it?"

"There was nothing to suggest anything but suicide."

Edwards thought for a moment. "Is this what you meant when you said that there had been too many deaths?"

"Yes," Wesson answered. "The deaths are all very straightforward—a heart attack, a suicide, and an automobile accident. But the fact that the deaths all occurred so close together is what is suspicious."

Edwards thought some more. "So, why didn't you tell me this? Why did you send me up to the lodge? You had already been there and knew what I would find."

Wesson shrugged. "I wanted a second opinion, a fresh set of eyes."

Edwards paused again. "I'm sorry. I guess I didn't see anything that you didn't see."

Wesson reached for a third file and handed it to Edwards.

"What's this?" Edwards asked.

"Read it."

When he had read it, Edwards asked, "A robbery?"

"Technically a break-in," Wesson said. "Lisa Thornton also called me directly about that. You remember that equipment room on the other side of the office? A few days after her father died, Lisa's caretaker, the Native man you encountered, found that the outside door on that room appeared to have been pried open. He told Lisa, and Lisa called me. The door frame had been pushed back together. I called in the robbery division techs and had the room dusted for prints, but the prints we found all belonged to the family or the caretaker. The thing is that there was no indication of when the break-in occurred. It could have been days or weeks or even months earlier."

"And nothing was taken?'

"No, a gun cabinet had also had its lock forced. It was the cabinet used for the family's personal hunting weapons, but nothing was missing."

"So how does that relate to the deaths?" Edwards asked.

"No idea," Wesson answered. "It might not relate at all."

Edwards thought for a moment. "So, why did we ask the lawyer to identify the body? You had met Lisa Thornton and could have done that."

"Yes, I had met her, but only a couple of times. I wanted a second opinion, just to be sure, someone who knew her better."

"Have you got any other files you want to show me?" Edwards asked.

"Don't be cynical," Wesson answered. "There are no more files." He paused and then held up a piece of paper. "Just this."

"What is it?"

"It is something that Annemarie Seymour told me. I'll read it to you. She said something like this: 'I knew he was gone, you know. The night he died, he visited me. All of a sudden, there he was, standing beside my bed. He had his pills in one hand and his hunting rifle in the other. I knew he was dead and had come to say goodbye. I called out his name, but he didn't answer. And then he was gone.'"

"That's weird," Edwards said.

"Not so weird," Wesson answered. "People who love each other deeply, who have lived a long time together, seem to have the ability to communicate without words. It is not at all surprising to me that John would come to say goodbye or maybe that Annemarie sensed he was gone and that produced a vision while she was half asleep."

"But wait a minute. If Annemarie told you that, if she made that statement, why isn't it in the file?"

"Because she didn't tell me that the day John died," Wesson answered. "It was later, when I went to investigate the robbery. I was already in my car, I was late for a meeting, and she told me that just before I drove away. I didn't think it was important at the time—I didn't know then that Annemarie was going to commit suicide—but as I was driving down the mountain, it occurred to me that I probably should have recorded it. So, I stopped the car and quickly scribbled down what I thought she had said."

"So, why didn't you put it in the file?"

"Because of the way I had recorded it, it wasn't an official statement. I had intended to type it up and show it to Annemarie to see if it was accurate and complete and then ask her to sign it. But she died before I could do that. It is merely hearsay now, and it didn't seem to matter once she had committed suicide."

"Did that statement make you question whether it really was suicide?"

"No," Wesson answered. "It confirmed it. It shows she believed in an afterlife and wanted to be with her husband." Wesson paused. "Did you happen to notice what was on Annemarie's bedside table when you went up to the lodge?"

"No," Edwards answered. "I just looked into that room and kept going on to Lisa Thornton's room because it didn't appear to be in use. But there was something about that in the file. A book, wasn't it?"

"A book called *Talking with the Dead: Communicating with Your Dearly Departed Made Easy.* And she had a number of similar books on her bookshelf. I think the proper term is that she was a spiritualist. After her death, I asked Lisa Thornton about the books. She said that Annemarie had had several miscarriages and she had started reading the books to see if there was some way she could communicate with her unborn children."

"I still think it's weird," Edwards asserted.

"I didn't say I agreed with her point of view," Wesson said. "I just wrote down what I remembered her saying."

"If that is the end of the reading material," Edwards said, "what's next?"

Wesson thought for a moment. "As I said, there have been too many deaths close together. I think we need to start digging deeper. Let's go see a doctor."

"A doctor?"

"The Seymour family doctor. His name is there in the report. And it was on John Seymour's pill bottle."

*****

The Northwest Medical Center was on Main Street, a couple of blocks from the hospital.

"We would like to see Dr. Perkins," Wesson told the medical assistant at the desk.

The assistant, a dark-haired, middle-aged woman, looked over the two men in RCMP uniforms. "He is seeing a patient." She paused. "Is this an...um...official visit?"

"Yes, it is," Wesson answered.

The two policemen sat in chairs in the waiting area while the assistant talked quietly on her phone.

A few minutes later, a white-haired woman came down the hall from the examination rooms, walking slowly with a cane.

24

The medical assistant stood up and nodded toward the policemen. Without a word, she led them down the hall to an office. The doctor was sitting behind a big oak desk and wearing a white lab coat. His hair was white but slightly longer than the lawyer's, and he moved more easily than his last patient.

He stood when they entered. When the assistant had closed the door, he said, "Good afternoon, gentlemen. What can I do for you?"

After introducing himself and Edwards, Wesson asked, "Am I correct that you were the family doctor for John and Annemarie Seymour?"

"Yes, I have been their doctor for many years. I took over their file from Dr. Goblonski when he retired a couple of years after I arrived here."

"What can you tell me about them?" When the doctor hesitated, Wesson continued. "We understand about doctor-patient confidentiality. We are not asking to see their medical records. We will get a court order if that becomes necessary. We just wanted to confirm that there is nothing suspicious about their deaths." Wesson paused. "For instance, I understand that you were treating John Seymour for a heart condition?"

The doctor relaxed somewhat. "Yes. Mr. Seymour had been a heavy smoker, and he was, frankly, getting to be an old man. He had had one previous heart attack, he had had a bypass surgery, but his heart was in a very fragile condition. He was a walking time bomb."

"So, it did not surprise you that he died of a heart attack?"

"Not in the least."

"Is it true that you had advised him to sleep on the main floor rather than upstairs?"

"Yes. As I said, his heart was quite fragile, and something as simple as climbing stairs could put enough strain on the heart to kill him."

"Have you read the autopsy report?"

"Yes. As his family doctor, I was able to access that."

"Was there anything in it that surprised you?"

"Not really."

"The investigation said that his medication was in the bedside table, he had gotten out of bed, but he had not taken any of the medication. Did that surprise you?"

The doctor paused. "That is hard to say. I would have thought that he would have had time to get to it. That is what it was there for. But who's to say? He might have fallen getting out of bed. And even if he had taken the medication, it likely would not have made any difference. It was a massive heart attack."

"Would you expect he would have had time to call for help or dial 9-1-1?"

"Not necessarily. Some people simply die in their sleep and never wake up."

Wesson paused and then asked. "What about Annemarie Seymour? I understand that you had prescribed an antidepressant called Xanifol and that she died of an overdose of that medication."

Perkins paused before answering. "In one sense, Annemarie was as fragile as her husband, but in her case it was her mind and emotions. Xanifol had helped her for some years. I think it especially helped ease her anxiety levels and relax enough to sleep. However, when taken in a large enough dose, it can be fatal."

"Were there underlying reasons for her depression?"

Perkins paused again. "I think Annemarie had had a hard life in some ways. Being stuck up there in that lodge could get pretty lonely. She had to work hard and didn't have much opportunity to have friends."

"The Seymours only had the one child?"

"That was another issue. They wanted more children, I think. Annemarie had several miscarriages and then couldn't get pregnant again."

"You have read her autopsy report too?"

"Yes."

"Anything surprising there?"

"No, not really."

"Had you seen Annemarie after John Seymour died?"

"No, I hadn't. She wasn't due for her regular appointment for another few weeks, and she didn't phone to make another one."

"In your opinion, would John's death have been enough reason to push her to take her own life?"

The doctor pondered that for a moment. "It is always hard to predict what goes on in the human mind. Losing John would have been a significant blow. Looking ahead to growing old away up there in that lodge with only her daughter could have been a bleak prospect. But, as I said, I hadn't seen Annemarie for some weeks. I couldn't really say anything definitive about her state of mind."

"What did you mean that it would have been a bleak prospect to live up there with just her daughter? Did Annemarie and her daughter not get along?"

"Oh, I am sure they had their tense moments, but, as far as I know, they were fairly close. I was thinking more that Annemarie had wanted more children, a bigger family. I think she would have liked to have had grandchildren. That might have happened when Lisa got married, but when Lisa's husband died soon afterward, that hope disappeared too."

"That raises another question," Wesson said. "What can you tell us about Lisa Thornton?"

"That puts me in a more difficult position," Perkins said. "It is one thing to tell you about patients who have died, but, as her doctor, what I know about Lisa Thornton is privileged information."

"I respect that, Dr. Perkins," Wesson said, "but that is why we are here. Lisa Thornton was killed in an automobile accident the night before last."

"Oh," Perkins said. "That is quite…shocking. I did not know." He paused. "That was the accident out on Mountain Road? That was Lisa?"

"Yes," Wesson said. "That information was not released earlier. The body was only formally identified late yesterday. The accident apparently happened the night before, but it was a single-vehicle accident, her SUV had rolled down an embankment, and it was not found until the next morning."

The doctor was silent, allowing that information to sink in.

Wesson continued, "Lisa Thornton's blood alcohol level was twice the legal limit. Do you know if she had a drinking problem?"

Perkins took a deep breath, "Mrs. Thornton would not have admitted she was an alcoholic, but I think she did drink quite heavily. She was in generally good health, and I didn't see her very often, but I had talked to her about it a couple of times. She...well, let's just say she told me to mind my own business."

"So, it didn't surprise you that she would have been driving under the influence of alcohol?"

"Well, I had never known about her driving while intoxicated, but patients don't tell their doctors everything."

"Would the deaths of her parents have led her to drink more?"

"Well, of course, that is certainly a possibility."

"What can you tell us about Lisa Thornton?"

"As I said, I have been her doctor for years. Lisa was a very pretty woman when she was younger, quite vivacious. She was popular and liked to party, I think. Nothing extremely wild, but growing up in the mountains surrounded by men probably influenced her."

"So, she drank heavily even as a young woman?"

"I wouldn't say heavily. She would drink at parties, but I suspect she started drinking more heavily after her husband was killed."

"What can you tell us about that?"

"Well, as I said, Lisa was an attractive woman and was popular with the American hunters who came to the lodge. And then she married one of them, Hunter Thornton. That was his name, an odd name for a man from New York City, but I think it was a family name. He was Hunter Thornton the second or third or something. As I said, Lisa Thornton was a good-looking young woman and quite vivacious. I think she might have fit well in a place like New York. Hunter Thornton was older than Lisa, in his thirties, I think, when they got married. I saw him once or twice in the office, for some minor ailments, but I didn't really know him well. He was tall and good-looking but not very dynamic. I was not surprised that he was attracted to Lisa. On her part, I think the prospect of marrying a wealthy man and moving to the big city must have seemed pretty glamorous."

"But that didn't happen?"

"Apparently not," Perkins said. "They got married here, and they spent some time in New York, but it seemed they spent more time here than there."

"Why was that?"

"I don't know. I would only be speculating. Maybe Lisa changed her mind about New York and got homesick. Maybe there were immigration issues. I suspect they would have moved there permanently in time, but then, when Hunter Thornton was shot, well, it put an end to her plans. That was quite distressing to Lisa, and I suspect it contributed to her drinking."

"Hunter Thornton was shot?"

"You didn't know?" Perkins asked.

"No," Wesson answered. "I knew her husband had died, but I didn't know how. Was it a hunting accident?"

"No, he was shot at the lodge by a young Native man. I'm surprised you don't know about it."

"That must have happened before I was posted here."

"In any case, it was quite devastating to Lisa. I don't think she ever fully recovered from the shock. She was never the same after that."

"In what way?"

"I guess you would say she was depressed. She became more serious, less outgoing. After experiencing New York City, it was quite a letdown to return to living here all the time."

"I see," Wesson said. "Dr. Perkins, do you know any reason why Lisa Thornton would have had a loaded hunting rifle with her in her vehicle when she died in the accident two nights ago?"

"No. I know she hunted occasionally, but that doesn't sound like something she would normally do."

"Could she have been frightened or paranoid?"

Perkins thought for a bit. "I don't know. As I said, I hadn't seen her since her parents died. I don't know anything about her recent state of mind."

*****

"That was interesting," Edwards said when they had come out of the office.

"What did I tell you back at the accident scene?" Wesson asked.

"Um..."

"If you want to understand what is happening in the present, you have to know what happened in the past. I want to know more about Hunter Thornton's death."

"I guess there would still be a file about that."

"Yes, and I want to talk to the lawyer again. It seems there were some things he didn't tell us."

*****

Lloyd Simmons's office looked the same. The same twenty-something receptionist directed them to the same small waiting area, and they waited for the same few minutes even though there was no evidence of any clients being in the office.

Lloyd Simmons stood while they entered, and while he spoke politely, he seemed even less pleased to see them than the first time.

"We are sorry to bother you again, Mr. Simmons," Wesson said, "but a couple of further issues have come up that we need to ask you about."

"Oh, yes?" Simmons answered. "And what are they?"

"For one thing, you told us that Lisa Thornton's husband had died, but you didn't mention that he had been murdered."

30

Simmons seemed to relax. "Well, that happened a long time ago. I didn't see how it could be relevant."

"Maybe," Wesson said. "But can you tell us what you know about it?"

"Of course. John Seymour had a habit of hiring Indians to work at the lodge. He said it made the lodge appear more authentic and exotic, particularly to Americans. I warned him that it was not a good idea and could lead to problems, but he refused to listen. He hired a young Indian—I don't remember his name—a boy with no experience or skills and probably limited English, and he gave him a job and a place to live. And how did the Indian show his gratitude? Hunter Thornton caught him stealing some of his personal possessions, right out of his room, and the boy shot him in cold blood."

"Was the young man caught and convicted?"

"Sergeant, surely you have the answer to that in your records." When Wesson didn't say anything, Simmons continued. "Yes, he was convicted and sent to prison, a good place for him. But Hunter Thornton was still dead."

"What impact did that have on the family?"

"They were devastated, of course."

"How about financially?"

"Well, it was a serious blow," Simmons said. "Among other things, Hunter Thornton had connections to a lot of potential clients in the United States. And the murder was very bad publicity for the lodge. In some ways, the lodge has never recovered what was lost."

*****

"Was that helpful?" Edwards asked when they were back in the car.

"Somewhat," Wesson answered. "Perhaps as much for what he didn't say as for what he said."

"What now?"

"We do what everybody seems to assume we have already done—start digging through the police files and find out more about that murder."

31

"Do you really think we are going to find something relevant to the recent deaths?" Edwards asked.

"I have no idea," Wesson answered. "But the key to a proper investigation is to look at all possible leads, no matter how unlikely."

*****

"For a murder investigation, that seems like a rather thin file," Edwards observed. "Maybe it wasn't as thorough as you would have done."

"Don't assume that," Wesson answered. "Every case is different. Maybe they followed every lead they had and there just weren't very many."

"Still, it is going to take us a while to go through this."

"What do you mean 'us'? I have other work to do. Let me know when you have finished."

"What do you expect to learn from this anyway? Hunter Thornton's murder case was solved and closed a long time ago."

"What I'm hoping for is some background information that might provide insight into why three members of the same family all died so close together."

"What if it is just a coincidence or for some other reasons not related to this old case?"

"If that's the case, then I hope the evidence shows that too."

Wednesday, May 30

It was the next day before Edwards reported back.

"Did you read the whole file?" Wesson asked.

"Not word for word." Edwards let out a long breath. "But almost."

"So, what was there?"

Edwards opened a notebook. "I can see why the file wasn't very large. It was a very straightforward case. There were three eyewitnesses, and they all told the same story. Hunter and Lisa Thornton were living in that main floor

32

bedroom connected to the office. The Thorntons and Seymours were all working in the office when Hunter Thornton went into his bedroom to get something. He left the door open. The others suddenly heard him say, 'What are you doing here?' Then there was a shot. Before they could move, a young Indian named Billy Timmishin ran out of the other door of the bedroom and along the hall into the lobby. Then he ran out the front door. He was still carrying the rifle."

"What kind of rifle?"

Edwards consulted his notes. "A Remington 7600, a hunting rifle. Ballistics later confirmed it was the murder weapon. Lisa Thornton and her parents ran into the other room. Hunter Thornton was dead on the floor, shot through the heart." Some drawers were open. Billy Timmishin worked at the lodge and was living in a cabin on the property. A Rolex watch and some other gold items belonging to Hunter Thornton were found hidden in Billy's room."

"Where was Billy?"

"When the police got there—remember it takes a good hour to drive up there—Billy was found wandering around on the property, still carrying the rifle. He was arrested without incident."

"What did the forensics say?"

"All straightforward. Hunter Thornton died of a single gunshot wound to the heart. Death would have been instantaneous. Billy Timmishin's fingerprints were all over the gun. There was some blood on both Lisa Thornton and John Seymour—they had both tried to help Hunter Thornton, but he was already dead."

"Were there any other witnesses?"

"No. There were seven clients staying at the lodge then, but they were out in the woods with a guide. None of them even heard the shot."

"I assume Billy Timmishin was interrogated. What did he have to say?"

"Yes, they interrogated him, but they hadn't gotten very far into the interrogation when he suddenly clammed up and demanded to see a lawyer. After that, they tried several times but never got another word out of him."

"Did he admit to killing Hunter Thornton?"

"No. They hadn't gotten that far. They were still covering the preliminary details when he stopped talking."

"Is that it?"

"Pretty much. As I said, it was very straightforward."

"Did you look up the trial transcripts?"

"Yeah, but I didn't read all that. It was mostly arguing about details. Billy Timmishin pleaded guilty to second degree murder. He got life with no chance of parole for twenty years."

Wesson calculated. "So, he would still be locked up?"

"Presumably, if he is still alive."

"What did the file say about who Billy Timmishin is?" Wesson asked.

"He was nineteen. He never had a father. He was raised by his mother on the local reserve. After she died, he got a job at the lodge. He had been there about a year."

"How did she die?"

Edwards sighed. "Suicide." He paused. "Let me guess. You want me to review that file too."

Wesson smiled. "It couldn't hurt."

"I've already pulled the file. I'll let you know what I find tomorrow."

Wesson smiled more broadly. "You're learning."

"What exactly am I looking for?"

"Oh, I don't know," Wesson said. "Anything that seems relevant. Who knows? Maybe Billy killed her too."

"Okay. Anything else?"

"Yes, was there anything more in the file about the Seymours and Lisa Thornton?"

"Not much. They all gave statements, saying pretty much the same thing. The investigating officers didn't report much about them. The family seemed to be in shock. They were sad, of course, and angry with Billy. That's about it."

Wesson sighed.

"So, have we learned anything that will help us with the current cases?" Edwards asked.

"Not as far as I can see." Wesson was silent for a moment. "Who were the investigators on the case?"

Edwards consulted his notes. "The lead was Angus McClintock, and the second was Pierre LaChance."

Wesson rubbed the back of his neck. "I don't know LaChance, but Angus was still on the force when I was posted here. He was a good investigator. In fact, I think he stayed in the area after he retired. I think it might be an idea to look him up and ask him for an opinion."

"Something else for me to do?" Edwards asked.

"No, that's something I'll do myself," Wesson said. "I can do it tomorrow while you're reading the other file."

Thursday, May 31

Angus McClintock was sitting on the front porch of a well-built log house, set among fir trees. As Wesson got out of his car and approached the porch, McClintock stood up. He was six feet tall, stood erect, and moved with a precise efficiency. He looked every inch a retired policeman.

"Good morning, Angus," Wesson said. "Thank you for agreeing to see me."

McClintock smiled. "No problem. I happened to have a small opening in my busy social calendar."

Wesson smiled back. "You're looking well, Angus. I'll try not to take up too much of your valuable time."

"So, how can I help you?" McClintock asked when they had sat down.

"I want to ask you, about an old case, the murder of Hunter Thornton," Wesson said.

"You're not reopening that case?" McClintock asked. "That was as simple a case as any I ever worked on."

"No, no, no," Wesson answered. "The murder came up in connection to another case, and I just wanted to fill in some background."

"What's the other case?" McClintock asked bluntly.

"I wouldn't mind getting your opinion on that case too," Wesson said. "But I'd like to ask you about the Thornton case first."

"Okay," McClintock said. "What do you want to know?"

"We've read the file, but can you just run through it quickly? I want to know if there is some aspect that I missed."

McClintock shrugged. "Sure. Like I said, it was a very simple case. When the call came in, LaChance and I were just coming back from dealing with another matter and were at the bottom end of that mountain road. We were the closest unit, it was urgent, and so we took the call. The call said that an Indian kid had gone wild and shot someone up at the lodge. We were told he was armed, so we made sure we were armored up, vests on."

"So, you already had an idea what the case was about before you got there?"

McClintock looked hard at Wesson. "We needed the warning about the kid having the gun, but that doesn't mean that we prejudged the case. We handled it professionally, by the book, from start to finish."

"Knowing you, I wouldn't have thought otherwise," Wesson said.

"You know the layout of the lodge?"

"Yes, I've been there," Wesson answered.

McClintock raised an eyebrow but continued. "Took us about an hour to get up there. Lights and sirens don't help much on that road. There's no traffic, just a winding gravel road."

Wesson nodded.

McClintock continued. "When we got close, we slowed down a bit, looking out for the kid with the rifle. I was driving. When we pulled into the clearing, I stopped so we could assess the situation."

"By the book," Wesson said.

"All of a sudden, we see the kid come out of the trees about a hundred feet away, still carrying the rifle, heading straight for us. We got out of the car, pulled our weapons, and took up positions behind the car doors. The kid was heading straight toward us, ahead of us but more toward LaChance's side. He had the rifle in front of him. He wasn't pointing it at us, but he wasn't pointing it at the ground either." McClintock paused. "Do you know LaChance?"

Wesson shook his head. "I don't remember him being here when I arrived."

"He got transferred. He was a good officer, but young and eager. It was probably one of the first times he had ever drawn his weapon. I was sure he was going to shoot the kid. I thought about it myself."

"What happened?"

"It was a very tense situation. I yelled out to the kid to put down the gun and stop where he was, but he just kept walking toward LaChance. We had no backup. It was the type of situation where cops get killed. LaChance had his gun pointed right at the kid, but the kid kept coming. Finally, when he was about five feet away, he held out the gun toward LaChance, not butt first but not barrel first either, sort of crossways, and LaChance took it. Technically, of course, it contaminated the rifle with LaChance's fingerprints, but at that point we were focused on surviving, not preparing a court case. In the meantime, as the kid approached LaChance, I had slipped around the front of the car and come up behind the kid. Before he realized I was there, I had cuffed him. He seemed shocked and surprised and then a little angry. He wasn't very tall, but he was wiry and stronger than he looked. LaChance and I managed to get him into the back seat of the cruiser after a bit of a struggle."

Wesson nodded. "That could have had a worse ending."

McClintock agreed. "For sure. That was only the beginning, of course. The crime scene techs went over the murder scene and the kid's cabin. The rifle was the murder weapon, and the kid's were the only legible prints on it, other than Lachance's. Some items belonging to Hunter Thornton were found hidden under the mattress in the kid's cabin. We looked at the case from every angle we could, but sometimes the obvious answer is the right one."

"A simple case," Wesson said. "Did you talk to Billy?"

"Of course. I took the lead and took the usual approach. I began by asking him how long he had worked at the lodge and how he had come to work there. He said that his mother had died about a year earlier, he had nowhere else to go, and so he had come and asked John Seymour for a job. I asked about his job. He said he did whatever needed doing. He cut wood, mowed that bit of lawn in front of the lodge, painted, that sort of thing. And he helped get the guns and vests ready for the hunters and the fishing gear ready for the fishermen— there was some good fishing in a couple of nearby lakes. That gave him access to the gun room, of course—he had a key. Then I began to move closer to the murder and what lay behind it. I asked him about the guests and the Seymours, about their cars and their gold watches. He admitted he was surprised at what these white men had. He had never seen that much wealth growing up. I asked him if that had made him want some of those things for himself. He said sure. And then it was as if it suddenly hit him what he had done and why. It was like he finally realized the trouble he was in. Then he just shut up, refused to say another word. After a bit, he said he wanted a lawyer. So, we got him a lawyer. After that, we tried to interrogate him a number of times, he might answer a preliminary question or two, and then he would clam up."

"What was your assessment of him?" Wesson asked.

"I don't know. It was hard to get a read since he didn't say much. I don't think he was very bright. I wondered about fetal alcohol syndrome, but he wouldn't talk to psychologists either, so that was hard to assess. I think he was unprepared for working at the lodge. He saw wealth he had never seen before, decided to help himself, got caught, and panicked. There weren't any other suspects, and in the end we let the evidence speak for itself. The case never even went to trial. The kid's lawyer got him a plea deal, and he took it."

"What about the family?" Wesson asked. "You interviewed them?"

"Sure. They seemed almost in shock about what had happened. They were pretty broken up, especially

Thornton's wife, Lisa, and they were angry. They felt betrayed after they had taken the kid in and given him a job. Their stories were pretty consistent. The only discrepancy was about the rifle. Lisa thought the kid must have brought it with him, and John Seymour wondered whether Hunter Thornton or Lisa might have accidentally left it in their room. He said they were sometimes a bit careless with the guns. But no one knew for sure. I think that's what got the charge reduced to second degree. If the rifle was already in the room, then the prosecutor couldn't be sure the murder was premeditated."

"Did you learn any more about the family? Did anything stand out to you?" Wesson asked.

"Not really. They were just a normal family. Sometimes the obvious answer is the right one. Why are you asking about all this anyway?"

"Well, what I really wanted was to see if you had any insights into the family," Wesson said. "You see, about a month ago, April 23, John Seymour died of a heart attack. On the evening of May 9, before or after midnight, Annemarie Seymour committed suicide, apparently deciding to join her husband. On May 27, Lisa Thornton was killed in a car crash. She was driving down from the lodge toward town, late at night, heavily intoxicated, with a loaded rifle on the seat beside her."

"Man, that is tragic," McClintock said. "But what's your question?"

"Look, none of these deaths is suspicious on the surface. It's just that they all happened so close together," Wesson said. "Do you have any insight into the family that would explain why they all died one right after the other?"

McClintock thought for a moment. "I don't know," he said at last. "The family was very close. They were badly traumatized when Hunter Thornton was killed, but they pulled together. Isn't the answer obvious? John Seymour dies of a heart attack. His wife is grief-stricken and decides to join him. Their daughter is left alone up in that remote lodge, grieving. She turns to alcohol for comfort and is killed while driving drunk. The deaths are connected, but in obvious ways."

"Yes, I know," Wesson answered. "But why was she driving to town late at night, and why bring the rifle?"

"She was grieving, and she was drunk. You wouldn't expect her to be acting rationally. Maybe she drove drunk on purpose, trying to kill herself like her mother had done. Maybe she brought the rifle along as Plan B in case her first attempt at suicide didn't work. Or maybe she was just drunk and paranoid and brought the rifle along for protection. Or maybe it was already in the car for some reason and she forgot it was there." McClintock paused. "Sure, the deaths coming so close together seems surprising, but there are obvious logical connections. I think you're looking for something that isn't there. If it quacks like a duck, most often it's just a duck. And it's not that unusual. Suicides often come in clusters, on the reserves, for instance. One person commits suicide, and others copy him, either because they're overcome with grief or because they're depressed for many of the same reasons."

"You're probably right," Wesson admitted.

*****

Wesson had called Edwards into his office. "What did you find out?" Wesson asked without preamble.

Edwards consulted his notes. "There were a cluster of five suicides on the reserve inside a couple of months, three teenagers and two single mothers. Lisette Timmishin was the fourth of the five and the second single mother. She was thirty-seven. Billy was her only child. The two of them lived in what the police report called 'a three-room shack' on the reserve. Lisette worked only sporadically and had no known romantic relationships. Her parents were still living in another house on the reserve, but she didn't have a lot of contact with them. She had some acquaintances but no close friends. She was known to be depressive and took an overdose of Xanifol, the antidepressant she had been prescribed by a doctor. She left a suicide note that said, 'I'm sorry, Billy. I couldn't stand it anymore. I got you this far. Now you'll have to make it on your own.'"

Wesson was about to interrupt with a question, but Edwards held up a hand and continued. "There was an actual police investigation, pretty thorough for a reserve suicide. A handwriting expert confirmed the note was her handwriting. Only her fingerprints were on the note and the pencil she used to write it and on the pill bottle and the glass of water she used to take them."

"Was anybody with her? Did she tell anyone else she was going to kill herself?"

"Nobody was with her. She hadn't told anyone what she was going to do, which wasn't considered surprising since she wasn't close to anyone. Her doctor said that she had been on the pills for years and that he had tried to convince her to go for counseling but she had refused. He was not surprised that she killed herself."

"Who found the body?"

"Her son Billy did," Edwards answered. "Found the body when he got off the school bus. It was his last day of high school. The school confirmed he was there all day. Before you ask, the medical examiner set the time of death between ten o'clock and noon. Billy left for school before eight and got home after four. No way he could have been involved."

Edwards paused, waiting for another question, but Wesson remained silent.

"Let me guess," Edwards said. "You want me to pull the files on the other suicides. I already pulled them and—"

"No," Wesson said. "I don't think you need to follow up on that avenue of inquiry—" He stopped. "You already read them? What did you find out?"

"Nothing," Edwards said. "I didn't read every detail, but I did give them a quick read. There were no apparent connections between the suicides other than the usual copycat factor in a cluster of suicides."

"That's fine," Wesson said. "As I said, I don't think you need to follow up on that any further." He paused. "Billy graduated from high school?"

"Apparently. Doesn't everybody?"

"Not everybody on reserves."

"So, we're done?"

"No," Wesson said. "There are a few more things I want you to follow up on. See if the medical examiner and forensics have come up with any new details on Lisa Thornton's crash." He paused. "Did Lisa Thornton have a cell phone?"

Edwards thought a moment. "I think there was one with her in the SUV."

"Follow up on that. See what was on it. Find out if other members of the family had cell phones. I wouldn't have thought they would be very useful up at the resort. There probably isn't any coverage up there."

"Okay."

"And dig up Billy Timmishin's school records." Wesson paused. "You said Billy Timmishin got life with no possibility of parole for twenty years. That means he must still be in prison somewhere. Find out where. If it is anywhere close, I might go and talk to him."

"Is that all?" Edwards asked. "We're doing a lot on this. I'm going to end up working into the weekend. Should we bring somebody else in to help us with this?"

"No, no," Wesson said. "I couldn't justify assigning more officers to investigating a simple automobile accident."

Monday, June 4

"Long weekend?" Wesson asked.

"And then some," Edwards answered.

"It's good you're young and eager," Wesson said.

Edwards scowled.

"What did you find out?"

"Not much new with forensics," Edwards said. "The medical examiner said blood alcohol testing is not necessarily as accurate when the person is already dead. You probably already knew that. But I guess they did some more tests, and they just confirmed the original conclusion that Lisa Thornton had a blood alcohol level of about point one-four. Also, tests on her liver indicated that she had been a heavy drinker, probably for at least a few years. There was some damage."

"Anything else?"

"I checked. Lisa Thornton did have a cell phone with her in the SUV. It was not password protected. I can see why. The log showed no record of any calls for several days. The directory listed only a few names—John Seymour, Annemarie—so, I guess they all had cell phones—her doctor and lawyer, a dentist, somebody named George Tessam—"

"That's the caretaker, remember?" Wesson said. "The man who could have shot you."

"Oh." Edwards resumed. "There was a mechanic, I think, and a few stores. She didn't seem to have any friends."

"Did you find out about cell service up the mountain?"

"I found out there is a tower up there. I asked the phone company how long it had been there and got shuffled from one office to another on the phone. For a communications company, they weren't very communicative."

"Did you ever find out anything?"

"Not from the phone company. So, I called Joe Morgan at Search and Rescue."

"Good thinking."

"Joe's been around a long time. He said the tower's been there for about twenty years. He remembers when they put it in. You'll never guess why."

Wesson thought a moment. "Because Moose Mountain Lodge convinced the phone company that its rich American guests needed cell service."

Edwards scowled. "Right. Joe thinks the phone company figured out they could make a lot of money from the roaming charges. Anyway, Joe says the tower has been helpful in some searches for lost hikers and hunters. And he says the phone company figured out that if they put it in the right place, the tower could also serve the Indian reserve. Joe says the company made a deal with the band office and just about every Indian has a cell phone now."

"First Nations, Edwards, First Nations."

"What? Oh. Anyway, Joe figured the phone company probably makes more from the reserve than from the lodge."

"Okay, good," Wesson said. "A public trustee has been appointed to take responsibility for the estate and is probably up at the lodge taking inventory. I want you to go back up there and see if you can find John and Annemarie's cell phones. Also, see if the trustee will let you take a look at the phone records for the cell phones and the lodge phone."

"Wouldn't I need a warrant for that?"

"Not necessarily. His job is to protect the interests of the family, and investigating their deaths could be considered part of that. See what he says anyway. Anything else?"

Edwards pulled a few sheets of paper out of a file he was holding. "I went to the school this morning and got a copy of Billy Timmishin's high school marks. The school didn't raise any objections. They said they had to keep the records for fifty years and they're public information."

"What did you find out?"

"Not much, as far as I can see. He was a solid B student with occasional As and Cs."

"Any comments?"

"Comments?"

"Yes. You know, something like 'Billy is a bright, inquisitive boy who likes to commit murder.'"

"There were no comments, just a list of marks."

"A transcript."

"Uh, okay," Edwards said, handing over the sheets. "They said they don't keep copies of the report cards this long."

Wesson looked through the papers. "Solid B student. No obvious favorite subjects or least favorite subjects."

"The school said that if he had talked to a counselor, there might be some information in the counselor's notes, but the counselors have changed since Billy was a student, and it would take a long time to look for them."

"Probably need a warrant for them anyway, if they did exist, and we don't have reasonable cause to ask for a warrant," Wesson said.

"Why does it matter anyway? Why do we care what marks he got in high school?" Edwards asked.

"It probably doesn't matter. I was just checking something that somebody told me and maybe trying to understand Billy Timmishin a little better." Wesson paused. "Anything else?"

"I found out where Billy Timmishin is now."

"Where?"

"Here in town."

"What?"

"Here in town."

"There's no prison here," Wesson said. "He was sentenced to life with no parole for twenty years. How did he get out early? Did he escape?"

"No. Apparently, his lawyer appealed the sentence or something. I haven't found out the details yet."

"Do you know where he is?" Wesson demanded.

"Sure. He's living at a halfway house called Prodigal Son House."

"Brother Bob's place," Wesson said.

"Do you know it?" Edwards asked.

"I know *of* it," Wesson said. "It's where a lot of parolees end up."

"Do you still want me to go back up to the lodge?" Edwards asked.

"Yes, but not just yet. First, we should go and see Billy Timmishin."

"Do you think he might have been involved in the deaths of Lisa Thornton and the Seymours?" Edwards asked.

"I don't see how," Wesson answered, "but the timing is certainly an odd coincidence. How long has he been in the halfway house?"

"About three months."

"So, he was in town at the time of all three deaths. Let's go talk to him."

*****

Prodigal Son House was a sprawling, old, two-and-a-half-story brick house on Hillman Avenue, a couple of blocks off Main Street. A veranda with a white railing ran across the front and along one side of the house. Century-old trees shaded a freshly mown lawn. There was no sign, but a three-foot wooden cross was fastened to the wall next to the front door. When Wesson rang the doorbell, curtains rustled, and they could hear the sound of quickly moving feet and firmly shutting doors.

"They don't seem overly fond of the police," Edwards said.

Wesson said nothing.

Moments later, the door was opened by a man of medium height with thinning black hair and a small goatee. He looked the policemen over but said nothing.

"Are you Brother Bob?" Wesson asked.

"No one here calls me that," the man answered. "I am just Bob, or Bob Hawthorne."

"I'm sorry," Wesson said. "We need to talk to Billy Timmishin."

"He's not here," the man said. Before Wesson could say anything further, Hawthorne said, "Perhaps we should talk in my office."

To the right of the door was a spacious living room. Straight ahead was a wide, curving staircase. But Hawthorne led them to the left, through a dining room with a massive table able to seat about twenty people. Beyond the dining room was an office about twelve feet square. They sat in front of an antique oak desk. Hawthorne closed the door and sat down in a swivel oak chair behind the desk.

"What do you mean Billy Timmishin is not here?" Wesson asked. "His parole requires him to stay here."

"Billy and a couple of the other residents are at a career counseling seminar downtown this morning."

"You let them go off on their own and trust them to go where they say they are going?" Wesson asked.

"This is not a prison," Hawthorne answered. "It is a halfway house. We help parolees transition from prison to life in society, and part of that is to gradually give them more trust and freedom. In this case, they went as a group and were told to stay together. It is an exercise in mutual accountability. They also know that the seminar is for their benefit."

Wesson nodded. "When will Billy be back?"

"The seminar goes until two-thirty. They should be back here by three," Hawthorne said. "Why do you want to talk to Billy?"

"We want to ask him some questions about a case we are working on," Wesson said. "We believe he knew the victims and might be able to give us some background information."

"And you think Billy might be responsible for the crime," Hawthorne said. It was not a question.

"It's possible," Wesson said, "but he's not necessarily a suspect. He knew the victims years ago. We don't have any evidence that he was in contact with them recently."

Hawthorne nodded. "Okay, but I should warn you that you might not get that much out of him. Billy is, to say the least, not very talkative."

"I suspect that is true of most of your residents," Wesson said.

"True, but Billy is more reticent than most."

"How many residents do you have here?" Edwards asked.

"We're licensed for fifteen, but we currently only have fourteen here. We expect to fill the last spot shortly. There are several candidates."

"You live here?" Edwards asked. "With fifteen criminals? How can you feel safe?"

Hawthorne smiled. "Do I feel safe? It's a lot safer for the whole community for those fifteen *former* criminals to be living here than it would be if they were out on the street."

"But why do you do it?" Edwards insisted.

"That's a long story," Hawthorne said. "My grandfather owned a jewelry store downtown. There was a man named Angelo, who had been released from prison. Angelo had nowhere to go. He had no job and no money. He had family and a few friends in the area, so he came back here after he was released, but they refused to have anything to do with him. He was living on the street. Somehow, he managed to get hold of a gun, and he decided to rob my grandfather's store. He killed my grandfather."

"That doesn't explain this," Edwards said, gesturing with his hand.

"I loved my grandfather," Hawthorne said, "and I needed to understand why he had died. Knowing my grandfather, I didn't think he would have risked his life to avoid being robbed. So, I went to see Angelo in jail. He said that he hadn't eaten in two days, he was nervous, his hand was shaking, and the gun just went off."

"And you believed him?" Edwards asked.

"Angelo was a small-time thief," Hawthorne answered. "He had no history of being violent. After he shot my grandfather, he passed out, either from shock or from hunger, or maybe both. He was still lying on the floor of the store when the police arrived. When I came to talk with him, he seemed deeply ashamed. He apologized to me for what he had done. He cried."

"It could have been an act," Edwards said.

"I don't think so. He pleaded guilty," Hawthorne said. "But I had my answer. My grandfather died because Angelo was hungry and had no place to go. I inherited my grandfather's house, and I decided to turn it into a halfway house for people like Angelo."

"How do you think your grandfather would feel about that?" Edwards asked. "Turning his house into a shelter for criminals like the man who killed him?"

"I think he would be very pleased," Hawthorne said. "I had been a street worker for the downtown gospel mission before that, and my grandfather had always been very supportive of my work. He was a devout Christian and practiced what he believed in."

"Is that why people call you Brother Bob?" Edwards asked.

"People do that as a way of making fun of what I do," Hawthorne said. "Or maybe it's because they heard that Grace Evangelical Church commissioned me to do what I do. But that didn't give me any title or formal license. It just means the church affirms and supports the work we do here."

"But after what happened to your grandfather, doesn't it make you even a bit uncomfortable to be surrounded by murderers like Billy Timmishin?" Edwards insisted.

"Do you know which criminals have the lowest rate of recidivism?" Hawthorne asked.

"What?" Edwards asked.

"Recidivism means returning to crime," Wesson interjected. "And the answer is murderers."

"Right," Hawthorne said. "For career criminals like thieves and fraudsters, who have been committing crimes for a long time before they got caught, it has become a way of life, and they often return to it. The same for drug addicts, alcoholics, rapists, and child molesters. They have trouble overcoming their compulsions. The same is also true for those in organized crime, who have committed multiple murders. But most murders are one-time events, committed on the spur of the moment, when anger takes over or an argument gets out of hand. The perpetrators get long sentences, and when they get out, they are older, they have had a long time to think about what they have done, and their adrenalin and testosterone levels are much lower. They don't usually reoffend. I think that's the case with Billy Timmishin. He had no history of violence, he got caught stealing, and he panicked. I'm not worried about him reoffending. But that's also why this house is here, to help people like Billy stay out of trouble."

"Very noble," Wesson said. "But we still want to talk with him. We'll be back at three. Make sure you don't warn him and he doesn't run off before we get here."

Hawthorne smiled. "As I said, this is not a prison. I can't lock Billy up. But the residents know that if they try to run and break parole, they will get sent back to prison. I expect Billy will be here."

"One more thing," Wesson said. "Can we see where Billy sleeps?"

"You can see where he sleeps," Hawthorne said, "but I can't let you search his room without a warrant."

"We won't do a search. We just want to see his room," Wesson said.

Hawthorne led them back through the dining room to a kitchen behind it. He opened a door, turned on a light and led them down a set of stairs into the basement. There was a laundry room and furnace room to one side, a big open space in the middle, and four bedrooms along the other side. Hawthorne led them to one on the end. It contained a single bed, a wooden chair, a battered chest of drawers, and a small bookshelf with a few books. There was a window near the ceiling. Wesson looked out. He could see a cracked sidewalk and lawn beyond it.

"Thank you," Wesson said, turning to go.

*****

"What do you think?" Edwards asked.

"I think we didn't find out very much that was useful," Wesson said. "Why did you ask all those questions about Brother Bob? None of that matters."

"I was curious," Edwards answered. "Someone told me that it is important for a policeman to be curious and ask questions."

"But Brother Bob's background isn't relevant to the case."

"I think someone also told me to find out everything you can because you never know what details might be important later."

"I think someone has selective hearing," Wesson said. "I also think you don't have time to go up to the lodge, find what we're looking for, and get back by three o'clock. Put that off until tomorrow."

*****

At three o'clock, Bob Hawthorne opened the front door.

"Is Billy Timmishin here?" Wesson asked.

"Over there," Hawthorne said, gesturing toward the living room.

As Wesson and Edwards approached, a young man stood up. He was of slightly less than average height, wiry, and clean-shaven, with a shock of unruly black hair.

"Billy Timmishin?" Wesson said. "I am Sergeant Wesson, and this is Constable Edwards. We would just like to ask you a few questions."

"I want my lawyer," Timmishin said. His voice was low, slow, and deep but clear.

"No, you don't understand," Wesson said. "You don't need a lawyer. You are not a suspect in anything. We just want to talk with you for a couple of minutes about some people you knew a long time ago. We don't know a lot about them and hope you can fill in some of their background."

"I want my lawyer," Timmishin repeated.

"Ah, Billy. You're not a suspect. This will only take a couple of minutes, and then we'll be gone. If you get a lawyer, we will have to do a formal interview down at the police station."

"I want my lawyer," Timmishin repeated.

Wesson sighed. "Okay. Who's your lawyer?"

Timmishin reached into the back pocket of his blue jeans and pulled out a business card, handing it to Wesson.

*****

Travis Battenfield arrived about fifteen minutes after they got back to the station. He was over six feet tall and looked to be about fifty, and his gray hair was tied back in a ponytail. He was wearing blue jeans, a plaid shirt, and a

51

buckskin jacket with fringed sleeves. He looked more like a lumberjack than a lawyer.

When he had been ushered into the interview room, he sat down beside Billy Timmishin and gave him a reassuring pat on the arm. Wesson turned on a tape recorder and began talking. "This is a simple conversation requesting information. However, at the request of the interviewee, Billy Timmishin, we are conducting it as a formal interview. Present are Sergeant Wesson, Constable Edwards, Billy Timmishin, and his lawyer, Travis Battenfield."

Wesson paused, leaned back, and looked at Timmishin. "Billy, as I explained earlier, you are not a suspect at this time. It is simply a request for information about some other people. I don't know whether you are aware that John and Annemarie Seymour and Lisa Thornton all passed away recently."

Wesson looked hard at Timmishin, but he showed absolutely no reaction.

Wesson continued. "Billy, you knew the Seymours and Lisa Thornton about fourteen years ago. What we're asking is if you can tell us anything you remember about them from back then, what they were like, what they were likely to do."

Timmishin said nothing, so Wesson asked, "Billy how did you come to know the Seymours?"

Timmishin surprised Wesson by actually speaking. "My mother told me that if I ever needed anything, I should go to the lodge and asked for help. So, I went to the lodge, and Mr. Seymour gave me a job."

"That was after your mother died?" Wesson asked.

Timmishin nodded.

"Did you know the Seymours before that?"

"I'd heard about them. I'd never talked to them."

"No big surprise there," Edwards mumbled.

"Were you surprised that Mr. Seymour hired you?" Wesson continued.

Timmishin shrugged. "No."

"How much were you paid?"

Timmishin shrugged.

"He was given fifty dollars a week plus room and board," Battenfield put in. "Far less than minimum wage. They claimed that they paid him a lot more but deducted his room and board, calculated according to what they charged the American hunters to stay there, three hundred dollars a night."

Wesson ignored the lawyer. "Billy, were you happy with your salary? Did you think you should have been paid more?"

Timmishin shrugged.

Wesson tried again. "How often did you talk with Mr. Seymour?"

Timmishin shrugged. "Every day."

"What did you talk about?"

"He told me what to do, and I did it."

"Did you talk about anything else?"

"No."

"What kind of man was Mr. Seymour? Did you like him?"

Timmishin shrugged.

"What kind of things did you do for Mr. Seymour?"

"Got the fishing poles ready. Cleaned the hunting rifles. Cut logs. Carried stuff. Drove the clients to fishing streams and to woods where they could hunt."

"What was your relationship like? Was Mr. Seymour happy with your work? How did he treat you?"

"He said I served him well."

"What about Mrs. Seymour? Did you ever talk to her?"

"No."

"Never?"

Timmishin remained silent.

"Did she ever mention talking to the dead?"

Timmishin shrugged.

"Did you know she was interested in that subject? Did she ask you what First Nations people believed about that?"

Nothing.

"We think Mrs. Seymour committed suicide. Was she the kind of person who would do that?"

Timmishin flinched slightly at the word suicide but said nothing.

"Come on, Billy," Wesson said. "Help me out here. I'm not blaming you for anything. I just want to know about Mrs. Seymour. Do you know anything that can help me?"

Timmishin shook his head.

"What about Lisa Thornton? What was she like?"

Timmishin shook his head. "Don't know. Didn't see her much."

"How much did she drink back then?"

Timmishin shrugged.

"Did you ever see her drinking or drunk?" Wesson almost shouted.

Timmishin remained silent.

"What about Hunter Thornton? What can you tell me about him?"

Timmishin pushed his lips tighter together and shook his head back and forth.

Wesson leaned back.

After a minute of silence, the lawyer spoke. "If you have no more questions, my client and I will be leaving."

"No more questions," Wesson said. "Of Billy. But I would like to ask you a couple of questions."

Wesson led the lawyer down the hall to his office.

"I would like to know, Mr. Battenfield. How did you get Billy out of prison?" Wesson asked. "He was sentenced to life with no parole for twenty years. He's only served thirteen."

"I'll spare you the legal details," Battenfield said. "The short answer is habeas corpus and compassionate computation. Billy was sentenced to life in prison, not sentenced to die. That would be cruel and unusual punishment. Billy has AIDS. He contracted it in prison. I suspect he was raped. That's a death sentence, which he should not have been given. As well, he was convicted of second degree murder, which means he should get no parole for ten to twenty-five years. His sentence was already at the high end of that range. He had served thirteen years, almost fifteen with the double credit for time served before the conviction. He had apparently been a model prisoner, not causing any problems and attending a lot of classes and counseling sessions. And the government is trying to mend relations with the First Nations community. The prosecutors didn't want to put a lot of effort into opposing my motion. Fifteen is what the sentence should have been to begin with."

"Maybe he didn't have a very good lawyer," Wesson said.

Battenfield smiled grimly. "Maybe. But I didn't have a lot to work with. The evidence was very strong. The prosecution had no worries about taking the case to trial." He paused. "You think you're not prejudiced, don't you? That you treat First Nations people the same way you treat white people? You're wrong."

"What makes you say that?" Wesson asked.

"You call me Mr. Battenfield. But you call Mr. Timmishin Billy."

Wesson paused for a few seconds. "I was trying to put him at ease so he would talk to me. I don't care if you talk to me."

"And how is that working?"

"I think that Mr. Timmishin only talks when he wants to."

"You got that right. Is that your conclusion, or did someone tell you that?"

"Someone told me that first," Wesson said. "But I have also discovered it for myself."

"Yes, Angus McClintock didn't get much out of Billy either."

"Look, Mr. Battenfield," Wesson said. "I am really not out to pin anything on Billy. I am just trying to figure out what happened to the Seymours and Lisa Thornton, if Annemarie would really kill herself, why Lisa Thornton drove down a mountain road at night drunk."

"You're asking me to tell my client to trust you?" Battenfield asked.

"Yes," Wesson said.

"My client doesn't trust you. He has no reason to," Battenfield said. "And Mr. Timmishin only talks when he wants to."

*****

"Did you learn anything from all of that?" Edwards asked.

"Obviously not," Wesson answered. "It is hard to turn a ship that isn't moving, and it is hard to guide a conversation when one person isn't saying anything."

"So, what's next?"

"Tomorrow, you go back up to the lodge, talk to the public trustee, and look for those cell phones. Also, ask for whatever phone records are available. And ask the trustee if he has a copy of the lodge's ownership history."

"Why that?"

"Just curious."

"Anything else?"

"Yes. Anything else you can come up with. Keep your eyes and ears open. Get whatever information the trustee will give you."

"That's a lot. You're not coming?"

"No, I have a pile of auto theft and robbery reports to go through tomorrow."

"Paperwork?"

Wesson paused. "Right. Paperwork."

Tuesday, June 5

"What did you find up at the lodge?" Wesson asked at the end of the next day.

"The trustee cooperated," Edwards answered. "He gave me a copy of the phone bills for the last couple of months, but I am not sure they tell us very much. There were three cell phones, for John, Annemarie, and Lisa. All are still active. I guess no one got around to cancelling John's and Annemarie's. We found Annemarie's phone in her bedside table. It needs charging, and the techs will have to bypass the password. But there was no sign of John's phone. Maybe they just junked it after he died."

"Or maybe they buried it with him, so Annemarie could still talk to him," Wesson said sarcastically. "Do the bills tell us anything at all?"

"Not really. Outgoing long distance calls are there for the lodge phone, but the cell phone bills just record total usage. They don't log individual calls."

"I'd still be interested in seeing the totals," Wesson said.

"There's just a few minutes."

"How many minutes, and what are the dates of the bills?" Wesson demanded.

Edwards consulted the pages. "The first bill ran to April 28. John used three minutes, Annemarie used thirteen minutes, and Lisa used thirty-seven minutes."

"Right. Not a lot."

"The most recent bill ran to May 26. John used nine minutes, Annemarie five minutes, and Lisa forty-three minutes."

Wesson thought a moment. "Do you see any problem with that?"

"Not really." Edwards shrugged.

"John Seymour used his phone for nine minutes between April 28 and May 27."

"So? That's not a lot."

"It is, considering that John had already died on April 23. He used the phone more the month after he died than he did the previous month when he was still alive."

"Oh, good point." Edwards paused. "Maybe Annemarie or Lisa used the phone after he died. Or maybe they gave the phone to that Indian caretaker?"

"Or maybe John did talk to Annemarie from the grave," Wesson said.

"Right," Edwards said.

"Anyway, check with George Tessam—the caretaker—to see if he did get the phone. Or if he knows who did."

"Okay."

"What's the number?"

Edwards gave it to him, and Wesson dialed. After a few moments, he hung up. "Straight to voice mail." Then he redialed, and this time he left a message. "This is Sergeant Wesson of the RCMP. This is an urgent matter. Please call me back at this number as soon as possible."

Wesson turned to Edwards. "Did you find anything else up at the lodge?"

"Not really," Edwards said. "Everything is pretty much the same. The trustee has been going over the lodge's finances, and they don't look great. The lodge is making money, but not much, just a few grand a year, hardly enough for three people to live on in the long run, even though the trustee said they were running most of their personal expenses through the lodge's books."

"The Seymours were seniors, though, and must have been receiving pensions."

"Yeah, but I think the trustee said only government pensions, no private ones. And he said the Seymours had no life insurance policies. He's still checking on Lisa."

"Anything else?"

"No."

"What about the lodge's ownership history?"

"The trustee said that's something he was going to check anyway but he hasn't gotten around to it yet. He said he would let us know when he has it." Edwards paused. "Why do you care anyway?"

"Just curious, being thorough," Wesson said. "And maybe a hunch too."

"What's next?" Edwards asked.

"I want to go back and see Brother Bob, and maybe talk to Billy again. There are some further questions I want to ask."

After a pause, Edwards asked, "Did you have a good day doing that paperwork on auto theft and robbery reports?"

"Scintillating," Wesson answered. "Did you know that there have been thirty-one cases of auto theft so far this year?"

"Thirty-one? Fascinating."

"And almost all of them were deemed joyriding incidents. All of the vehicles have been recovered except one, but three were found burned. Four others had parts removed."

"So, if your car needs a new muffler, you steal a car of the same make and model and move the muffler from the stolen car to yours?" Edwards asked.

"Sure. Everybody wins. You get a replacement muffler, and the other guy gets a new muffler."

"Partially paid for by the insurance company," Edwards suggested.

"Maybe, depending on the deductible. But, as I said, most of the thefts were joyrides. This one is typical." Wesson held up a file. "Paul Chambers left his pickup truck parked in front of his house on Hillman Avenue. He gets up on the morning of Monday, April 23, and discovers the truck missing. He reports it to the police. A few hours later, the truck is found a few blocks away, parked on Main Street. Mr. Chambers can't remember how many miles were on the truck when it was stolen. He can't remember how much gas was in the truck, but he thought it might have been more than the half a tank that was in the truck when it was recovered. On the other hand, he wasn't sure. He thinks the truck looked a little dirtier when it was found, but again he can't be sure. So, did somebody go for a joyride? Did somebody steal the truck and only drive it a few blocks in order to steal gas? We don't know. There were no fingerprints on the truck other than the owner's."

"The thief was smart enough to wear gloves."

"Right. No parts seem to have been removed from the truck, and there was no damage."

"No damage? Not even a broken window? The truck wasn't hotwired?"

"Oh, no. Mr. Chambers conveniently left the truck unlocked and the key under the front floor mat."

"Because in a small town like this, there is very little crime and a man can trust his neighbors."

"Precisely."

Wednesday, June 6

When Wesson rang the doorbell, he again heard a faint scurrying, like mice fleeing for cover when a light is turned on. He was about to ring again when Bob Hawthorne answered the door.

"You're like a persistent salesman who keeps coming back even though no one wants what he is selling," Hawthorne said.

"Thank you," Wesson answered. "Persistence is a key ingredient of good police work."

Hawthorne was silent for a few moments. "Let me guess. You want to see Billy Timmishin? He is not here. He is back at the career counseling seminar today."

"I can see Billy later," Wesson said. "I actually wanted to talk to you."

"Sure. I can avoid answering your questions as well as Billy," Hawthorne said. "Come in. We had better go to my office."

When they were seated in the office, Hawthorne asked, "What do you want to know?"

"You said you could avoid answering questions as well as Billy. I assume that means you think Billy didn't answer my questions. Does he not answer your questions?"

Hawthorne smiled. "Billy insisted on having his lawyer present when you talked to him. He didn't want to talk to you, and he was very careful about what he said. Am I right?"

"Okay. Does Billy talk much here?" Wesson asked.

"He probably says more here than he would say to you, but, as you have no doubt discovered, Billy does not talk a lot. He contributes to group discussions but only when he has something significant to say. He will answer questions when asked, but he hardly ever initiates a conversation. He is generally one of the quieter and more pleasant of our clients, but he tends to keep to himself a lot."

"I would also like to know a bit more about the arrangements here," Wesson said. "How easy would it be for one of your clients to sneak out without you knowing about it?"

Hawthorne pondered that question. "As I told you before, this is not a prison. We do not physically restrain our residents. However, we keep them pretty busy. They have chores to do around the house. We have counseling sessions and meetings. We send them out for courses like the one Billy is taking now. They do volunteer work at some charities, and we sometimes get them some paid work, doing odd jobs. Some go to AA meetings. We take them to church on Sundays."

"Church?" Wesson interjected. "Isn't that a violation of their rights? What if they belong to some other religion or are atheists?"

"It is part of the program," Hawthorne answered. "Our residents know that coming in. They don't have to come to our program. There are other halfway houses."

"But you get government funding, right? Doesn't the government object to that?"

"Our residents are on social assistance, welfare. We don't get any other government funding. The government was hesitant at first, but we get results. Parolees who come here have a lower rate of recidivism than those in the other halfway houses in the area. Besides, we are a cheaper option since we don't ask for government grants. There are not a lot of people lining up to run halfway houses."

"Then how do you get paid?" Wesson asked.

"We have a board of directors. We do some fundraising, mostly in local churches..."

"Never mind," Wesson interrupted. "So, you keep your residents busy during the day. What if they say they are going to an AA meeting and go somewhere else?"

"They usually go in groups, especially at first. And we check with the people running the programs to make sure they show up."

"What if they don't?"

"It doesn't happen often. If they don't follow the rules, their parole can be revoked. We have had a few over the years who have tried to run off. They all ended up back in prison."

"What about at night?"

"The residents are normally expected to be in their rooms by eleven. The outside doors are locked," Hawthorne shrugged. "This is not a prison. It is possible for someone to sneak out, but they would be taking a chance that another resident might see them or they would leave a door unlocked. And I would know if they weren't here for breakfast."

"Billy's room is in the basement. Could he have crawled out his window, for instance?"

Hawthorne pondered that. "It's possible, I suppose. Billy is small and might fit through. He might be heard though."

"Do you have any way of recording what a specific resident was doing on a specific day?"

Hawthorne reached for a binder beside his desk. "What do you have in mind?"

"You keep detailed records?"

"There is a daily schedule which outlines housekeeping duties, meetings, seminars, and who is supposed to be where. At the end of the day, I take a copy of the schedule and make note of any changes, problems, developments, or achievements. It can be useful. You want to know something specific?"

"Yes," Wesson answered, pulling out a notebook. "Can you tell me what Billy Timmishin was doing on Sunday, April 22, and Monday, April 23?"

"Why those dates?" Hawthorne asked. "What are you really after? Do you suspect Billy of committing a crime?"

"It's a shot in the dark," Wesson answered. "Just routine checking and filling in blanks. Do you know about Billy's crime, the one that got him sent to prison?"

"He shot a man up at Moose Mountain Lodge, the son of the owner, I think."

"His son-in-law, actually, a man named Hunter Thornton," Wesson said. "In the last few weeks, Hunter Thornton's wife and her parents have all died, separately. I'm just puzzled. I don't know if there has been foul play. I don't know if the deaths are connected. And I have no idea if Billy Timmishin might have been involved, if he had any contact with any of them, or even if he might know something about the family that would help us figure out what happened. We are checking every possible lead we can think of, and, because of what happened in the past, Billy is one of them. I could be completely wasting my time, and yours."

"I see," Hawthorne said, flipping pages. "Here we are. Sunday, April 22. Billy went to Grace Evangelical Church in the morning with the other residents. He was on clean-up duty after lunch. Sunday afternoon was free time. Some of the senior residents, those who have been here a while and have earned some trust, went for a walk around the neighborhood, and Billy went with them. We had an informal house meeting after supper, mostly just a general discussion. Everyone was there. That's it. It was a quiet day."

"What about the next day, Monday?"

"We had group counseling in the morning. Everyone was present, except for one resident who had a medical appointment. I made some notes on what some of the others said, but there was nothing from Billy. That was not unusual. He was again on clean-up after lunch. Some of the others had various meetings in the afternoon. Billy didn't, so he was part of a group doing some house cleaning, vacuuming, that sort of thing. He had a scheduled slot for doing laundry that evening. So, another uneventful day."

"You don't have any notes on his mood, whether he was tired or sick?"

"There is nothing in the notes. I do make note of that sort of thing, but apparently nothing stood out."

"What about Wednesday, May 9?"

Hawthorne flipped some more pages. "Again, we had group counseling in the morning. In the afternoon, Billy was part of a work crew we sent out to help an elderly couple clean up their yard. Billy and another resident cooked dinner that evening. We had a movie night and discussion in the evening." Hawthorne flipped the page over. "Oh, right. I do know where Billy was that night. I was woken up about two-thirty by a loud bang outside. The man who lives across the road, Artie Goddard, had come home drunk and crashed his car into the doorframe of his garage. I remember it because Mr. Goddard had tried to start a petition to get our operation here shut down. He said it would increase the crime rate in the neighborhood. The irony was that he was the one who got arrested."

"So, what does that have to do with Billy? Was he involved in the accident?" Wesson asked.

"No. But I was already awake, and I wanted to make sure none of our residents had been involved, so I did a bed check. Everyone was here, including Billy. And yes, I checked faces, making sure none of them had sneaked out and left a pile of pillows under the covers."

"What about the next day, May 10?"

Hawthorne flipped the page. "Group counseling in the morning. In the afternoon, Billy was on another work detail, helping another senior with yardwork. He helped cook dinner..."

"Yeah, okay." Wesson interrupted. "What about Sunday, May 27?"

Hawthorne turned more pages. "Again, Billy went to Grace Evangelical Church in the morning with the other residents. They stayed for a potluck lunch at the church afterward. Free time in the afternoon. In the evening, a couple of the residents had organized a euchre tournament. I allowed them to finish late, after curfew, at eleven-thirty."

"Billy participated?"

"Yes, but he didn't win. I think his team was eliminated by about ten."

"And the next day?"

Hawthorne turned the page. "Nothing unusual. Group counseling in the early morning, and then he started the employment counseling course that day. He was on clean-up duty for supper. I have no notes on his mood that day."

Wesson was silent for a moment.

"Now, are you satisfied Billy did not have anything to do with those deaths you are investigating?" Hawthorne asked.

"I never said he did," Wesson said. "What about phone calls?"

"The residents are not allowed cell phones. They are allowed to use the house phone on a very limited basis."

"Did Billy use the house phone?"

Hawthorne picked up another binder. "I don't recall that he has ever made any outgoing calls, but he has received a few." Hawthorne began running his finger down the pages, "Let's see. April 15, seven minutes. April 25, ten minutes. May 1, eight minutes. May 8, two minutes. May 12, five minutes. May 17, eight minutes. May 25, three minutes. May 30, twelve minutes."

"Billy talked that long?"

Hawthorne smiled. "I suspect Billy did more listening than talking."

"Who called him? I didn't think he had any close relatives."

"The same person," Hawthorne said. "Rick called him. Rick was one of our first graduates, about ten years ago. Rick works for a delivery company. He does the early shift, gets off work in mid-afternoon, and then many afternoons and evenings he runs a sports and activity program for Native kids."

"Why did he phone Billy?"

"They had grown up together on the reserve and reconnected after Billy moved in here."

"How can I get in touch with him?"

Hawthorne smiled. "Rick is bringing a group of Native kids to talk with some of our residents after school this afternoon."

"Is that a good idea?"

"It's a very good idea," Hawthorne said. "Some of these kids think it is fun to drink, get high, and steal things. It's like a game to them. When they meet our residents and hear what prison is really like, it takes away the glamour. It's a reality check."

*****

"This is Rick."

"Rick, this is Sergeant Wesson of the RCMP. I would like to talk with you. Where are you?"

"I'm doing deliveries. What's this about?"

"You are not in any trouble. It has nothing to do with you. I just want to ask you a few questions about Billy Timmishin. It's not really about Billy either. I'm hoping he can give me some background information for a case I'm working on, and I would just like to know a little bit more about Billy, where he might be coming from, so I can understand him better."

There were a few moments of silence. Wesson wondered if Rick might have hung up. Then he spoke.

"How long will this take?" Rick asked.

"Just a few minutes, maybe half an hour at most."

"Okay. I should be finished work a little after one."

"Do you want me to meet you there?" Wesson asked.

"No," Rick answered. "I don't need my boss thinking the police are after me."

"I understand," Wesson said. "Do you want to come in to the police station?"

"Sure."

"Do you know where it is?"

"Yes." Rick paused. "I've made deliveries there. I should be there about one-thirty." He paused again. "But I need to pick up some students at two-thirty. I run a kids' program..."

"Yes." Wesson interrupted. "I am aware of your appointment at Prodigal Son House. I talked with Bob Hawthorne this morning. We should be done in time."

*****

Rick was dressed in running shoes, blue jeans, and a sweatshirt. He was about Billy's height but wider and healthier looking. He was sitting in a chair in front of the table.

"Thank you for coming in," Wesson said as he came into the room. "I am Sergeant Wesson." He held out his hand, and after a moment Rick shook it. "We are in an interview room," Wesson continued, "but this is not a formal interview. This is just a quiet place to talk. We are not recording this, but I may take a few notes." He pulled out a notebook and laid it on the table. "As I said before, I am investigating some incidents involving people that Billy might have known, and I just want to see how reliable his impressions of them might be. I understand you've known Billy for a long time?"

Rick was silent a moment before answering. "Sure. We're the same age and grew up together on the reserve. We were friends."

"But you're not friends now?"

"We're back talking to each other, but we lost touch with one another for a few years."

"Why was that?"

Rick took a deep breath. "You know my history, that I was in prison?"

Wesson smiled. "I looked up your record, yes, but that is not why I asked you to come in."

"But you know what I went to prison for?"

"Your record says dangerous driving."

"Yeah. When I was a teenager, in high school, I did what a lot...well, some of the other guys were doing. We would get some beer, steal a car, and drive around. When we were done, we would ditch the car, maybe burn it."

"To get rid of the evidence?"

"Yeah, maybe, but sometimes just because we felt like it. It was fun." Rick paused. "But one night we had an accident. I was driving and hit another car. A woman was injured. I was banged up, not too bad, but I was out for a while. When I came around, the other guys were gone, and the cops were there. The woman was badly hurt. I got three years and was in prison for two."

"Was Billy one of the other guys in the car?"

"No, that's the thing you need to know. Billy wouldn't go along with stealing cars. That's why we stopped being friends. We were doing different things and just weren't together anymore."

"Billy never did anything wrong?"

Rick waved a hand. "Billy was...I think the best word would be compliant. That's how he got along. That was the way he chose to survive in life. Billy lived with his Mom. She had a band house and got a band allowance. She gave him a place to sleep and fed him, but that's about all she ever did for him. Billy never complained, just accepted that's the way it was. He accepted the way things were and went along with it. He did what he was told. He *complied.* They told him he had to go to school. He went to school. They told him to study math. He studied math. They told him to study English. He studied English. They told him to study science. He studied science."

"But his mother died," Wesson said. "How did that affect him?"

Rick shrugged. "I'm not sure. We weren't hanging out together by then. I went to see him after she died and suggested we get some beer. I thought it might help to just get drunk. But he refused, said he didn't need it. I said we could steal a car and ride around for a while, but he said it wasn't right to steal somebody else's car. He said the worst thing anybody could do was to have somebody trust you and then betray them. He had this sense of...I don't know...justice maybe, that people should be trusted to do the right thing and that if they didn't, they deserved to be punished really bad. I think maybe it was the betrayal of trust that bothered him the most."

"How did you react when he said that?"

"That sure wasn't how I was living my life. I took off then. I never saw him again for years. Next thing I heard was that he'd gone off and got a job at the hunting lodge."

"Was he mourning his mother when you saw him?"

Rick shrugged. "It was hard to know with Billy. He never said very much. I think he loved his mother, but they can't have been real close. She never showed him any affection that I saw."

"But you never saw him much after that?"

"Never saw him at all, until recently. He was living at the lodge, and a couple of months later I got arrested. I didn't have time to worry about what Billy was doing."

"So, you don't know anything about Billy's arrest?"

"I was already convicted and in prison by then. Didn't even hear about it till a long time after. We weren't in the same prison."

"I don't believe you. If Billy never did anything wrong, if he was always compliant and had such a strong sense of justice, why did he steal from his employer and commit murder?" Wesson demanded sharply.

"I don't think he could have," Rick answered evenly. "That's not like Billy. I don't think he did it."

"He pleaded guilty!" Wesson almost shouted.

"His lawyer pleaded guilty in a white man's court. That doesn't mean he did it. I pleaded guilty."

"And you were guilty," Wesson said.

"Yeah, but my lawyer never asked, just told me to take the plea bargain. I don't think Billy did it."

"He was caught red-handed, just like you were."

Rick just shrugged.

"You're talking to Billy again, now, right? Have you talked about that? Did you ask him if he did it?

"No, we haven't talked about that," Rick said. "We're just starting to talk again, get reacquainted."

"What do you talk about?"

"Just normal stuff, how he's feeling, how he's getting along at the house, what he is planning to do for a job."

"What does he say?"

"Billy doesn't say much. I end up doing most of the talking."

"What do you talk about?"

"My life. What I'm doing. What's happening on the reserve."

"Do you ever talk to him about what's happening at Moose Mountain Lodge?"

Rick shrugged. "A little bit."

"You would know, wouldn't you?"

"What do you mean?"

"You're Rick Tessam. The caretaker at the lodge is George Tessam. Is he your father?"

"My uncle."

"Do you talk to him often? Does he tell you what is going on there?"

"Yeah, we talk every week or so."

"What about?"

"We talk about life on the reserve and family issues. My father is dead, you know."

"No, I didn't know," Wesson said. "Do you talk about what's happening at the lodge? Did you talk about the recent deaths, for instance?"

Rick shrugged. "A little bit, mostly in relation to what the deaths will mean for Uncle George's job."

"Did you pass that information on to Billy? Did you tell him that John and Annemarie Seymour and Lisa Thornton had died?"

Rick nodded. "Yeah, I mentioned the deaths to Billy. He knew those people. I thought he might be interested, but he wasn't, at least as far as I could tell. I think he might be trying to put that part of his life behind him."

"Like you did?"

"What do you mean?"

"You were at Prodigal Son House, and that means you would go to church. I suppose you 'found Jesus' and 'got saved'?"

Rick bristled. "When I came to Prodigal Son House, I was angry and bitter. I had no job, no ambition, and no direction or purpose. Now I have all of those. What do you think?"

"Is that what you want for Billy?"

"Yes, without a doubt."

"Is he buying what you're selling?"

Rick was silent for a bit and then answered. "Billy doesn't talk much. It's always hard to know what he is thinking."

"Did Bob Hawthorne suggest you talk to Billy?"

"Sure, but I was glad to do it. I'm glad I'm doing it."

"Do you have a car?"

"I have a pickup."

"Did you kill John Seymour?"

"I understood he had died of a heart attack."

"You didn't answer the question."

"No, of course, I didn't kill John Seymour."

"Did you drive Billy up to the lodge so he could kill John Seymour?"

"No, of course not."

*****

"What do you think?" Edwards asked.

"I don't believe Billy Timmishin is compliant," Wesson answered. "Pick him up and bring him in. And tell that lawyer of his to get in here too. Save Billy making a phone call."

*****

"Mr. Timmishin, as we said before, you are not here as a suspect but as a witness," Wesson said. "This is just an interview to shed light on some people that you knew a long time ago. Now, can you tell me again how it was that you started working at Moose Mountain Lodge?"

Billy Timmishin looked intently at the policeman, as if he was assessing the situation. Then he said, "My mother told me that she had worked at the lodge when she was young and if I ever needed money, I should go there and ask for a job. That was a few days before she died."

Wesson sensed a flutter of movement in his peripheral vision, but when he stole a quick glance at Battenfield, the lawyer was sitting immobile and stone-faced.

"Were you surprised when Mr. Seymour offered you a job?" Wesson asked.

Billy shrugged. "No."

"What was your job?"

"I told you. Whatever needed doing."

"Can you drive a car?"

The sudden change in direction did not elicit any visible reaction from Billy since he always paused before answering a question. "My mother never had a car when I was growing up. I've never had a driver's license."

"Might I remind you, Sergeant, that my client has been in prison for more than thirteen years?" Battenfield put in. "That hardly gave him an opportunity to develop his driving skills. And why are you even asking about that?"

"It doesn't matter," Wesson answered. He turned back to Billy. "What can you tell me about your employers, the Seymours and Thorntons?"

"I worked for them. I always did what they told me to do," Billy answered.

"But what were they like?" Wesson persisted. "Were they nice or nasty? Were they fair or unfair? Did they talk a lot or not much?"

Billy said nothing.

"Did they get along with each other? Did you ever see them argue?"

Billy showed no sign of answering.

"Did you think Lisa Thornton was pretty?" Wesson's voice had risen a bit.

Billy remained silent.

"Why did you kill Hunter Thornton?" Wesson shouted, slamming his hand down on the metal table.

Billy remained silent, immobile.

"Did you kill John Seymour?" Wesson was leaning across the table shouting into Billy's face.

Billy did not flinch. But Wesson finally saw a reaction. Behind the impassive mask on his face, Wesson could see a flicker in the eyes, a flash of anger and hatred. Wesson had seen that look on many faces in interview rooms such as this one.

Travis Battenfield stood to his feet, glaring at Wesson. "That is quite enough, Sergeant. My client is here as a witness, not a suspect. You have no right to attack him. This interview is over!"

Battenfield motioned to Billy to stand. The two of them walked to the door. After Billy had gone out into the corridor, Battenfield turned back into the room and took a step toward Wesson.

"What the heck was that?" Battenfield said in a low but angry voice. "What did you think you were doing?"

"Talking nicely to Billy wasn't getting me anywhere," Wesson said evenly. "He wasn't telling me anything. I wanted to see what would happen if I took a harder approach."

"Yelling at Billy Timmishin won't make him talk," Battenfield said.

"What will it make him do?" Wesson answered.

*****

"What were you trying to do?" Edwards asked when they had gone.

"I was trying to get a reaction, get past that silence of his," Wesson answered.

"That didn't get him talking."

"No, but it did get a reaction. Did you see the anger on his face? When he is pushed, I believe Billy Timmishin is quite capable of murder."

Monday, June 11

Wesson looked up from his desk as Edwards walked through the door.

"Good morning, sir."

"Something new?"

"Yes, there is," Edwards answered, waving a sheaf of papers. "The trustee finally sent over the information I asked for. There are pages and pages of it."

"Accountants," Wesson said. "You ask them a simple question, and they give you a finely detailed and perfectly accurate hundred-page answer that leaves you more confused than you were before."

"Right," Edwards said.

"Find anything interesting there?"

"I've just started going through it all. I've found a couple of things you might want to know. There are all kinds of financial records, but one of them is a kind of summary of the lodge's finances over the last twenty years."

"Let me see" Wesson said. He perused the document and then looked up. "Interesting. The lodge has not been a huge financial success over the last few years."

"No," Edwards agreed. "And this is also interesting. Apparently, the lodge has a line of credit for operating expenses, and it has been deeply in the red for quite a while." He handed it over.

Wesson read it and then leaned back in his chair. After a moment, he said, "I think it's time I paid another visit to Lloyd Simmons. The Seymours' lawyer should have known all of this, and he never told us about it."

"To be fair, I don't think I asked him."

"No, but I am going to ask him."

"Should I come with you?"

"No," Wesson said. "I'll go by himself. You keep looking through the rest of the documents."

"Thank you," Edwards said. "It is going to be so much fun."

"Just think," Wesson said. "If you keep progressing the way you are, maybe in thirty or forty years, you will get promoted to sergeant and you will be able to give the worst jobs to some other poor schmuck."

"Right," Edwards said, turning to leave. "Thanks for the encouragement and glowing affirmation of my career prospects."

*****

After another wait on the black leather couch in the small waiting room, the twenty-something receptionist showed Wesson into Lloyd Simmons's office. The lawyer stood behind his desk but again did not offer to shake hands.

"This is becoming tedious," he said.

"Most police work is tedious," Wesson answered. "Thanks for your concern."

This produced a momentary pause before the lawyer continued, "What can I do for you today, officer?"

"I want to talk to you about the finances of Moose Mountain Lodge." Before the lawyer could object, Wesson said, "I should tell you that the public trustee has given us copies of the financial records."

"Then what do you want from me?" the lawyer growled.

"The records tell us what. They don't tell us why," Wesson said. "The lodge was doing reasonably well, bringing in considerably more than a million dollars a year and producing a pretty good income for the family. But then the lodge suffered a significant drop in revenues, and revenues have continued to decline. Revenues were only a couple of hundred thousand last year, and the lodge barely broke even. Can you help me understand the reasons for the decline?"

"That should be obvious," Simmons said. "When that Indian kid shot Hunter Thornton, it was a serious blow to the reputation of the lodge. American hunters, particularly those who knew Thornton, were not interested in coming to a place where they might be shot by Indians. Remember that the lodge had marketed itself as an authentic wilderness lodge partly staffed by Indians. The lodge got some bad reviews, and its ratings by adventure magazines and websites dropped accordingly. You have to also understand how traumatizing the murder was for the whole family, especially Lisa, to have to watch her husband bleeding to death on the floor of their bedroom. It was hard on John Seymour too, since he was the one who hired the Indian kid. He had a great sense of betrayal and even guilt. If Hunter Thornton had remained alive, there is a good chance he could have turned Moose Mountain Lodge into a major destination for hunters. With him gone, Lisa traumatized, and the Seymours getting older, they just didn't have the energy to keep the place going. In a sense, they had lost their vision and hope for the lodge—and all because of that ungrateful Indian kid."

Wesson was silent a moment, as if he was letting all of this sink in. "The public trustee also gave us a summary of the line of credit for the lodge. At the beginning, the lodge might dip into the line of credit during the off season and then pay it all off during hunting season."

"So?"

"So, about thirteen years ago, the line of credit suddenly shot up to about a hundred and fifty thousand, and it has stayed there ever since. It currently sits at a hundred and seventy-one thousand. Can you tell me why that is?"

"I already told you," the lawyer said testily. "When the Indian kid shot Hunter Thornton, it was a serious blow to the lodge, and they had to start borrowing money."

"I don't think that fully explains it," Wesson said. "Why did the line of credit have that one big jump and then level off again?"

The lawyer was silent.

"Do I have to remind you," Wesson said, "that your clients are dead? There is not much point in protecting their privacy now."

Simmons sighed. "I suppose you would get the information from the public trustee eventually anyway." He was silent for a bit and then sighed again. "I guess you could say it was always about money."

"You mean Billy Timmishin killed Hunter Thornton for money?"

"No, what the Indian kid stole was small change. I was talking about larger sums of money."

"I don't understand."

"Lisa Seymour was a beautiful young woman, and Hunter Thornton was a sophisticated New Yorker. I don't doubt that they were in love with each other, but there were some pretty sharp calculations involved too. John and Annemarie encouraged the relationship because they thought it would give them more access to rich American clients. For Lisa, the thought of moving to a luxury condo in New York was pretty appealing."

"Yes, I had deduced that might be the case."

"But the financial considerations went both ways. Before they got married, Lisa and Hunter Thornton signed a detailed prenuptial agreement. Hunter's lawyers drafted it, and I didn't see it until later."

"Okay."

"The agreement stated that if Hunter Thornton died, Lisa would only get half of his estate. The rest would go to Hunter's parents. If they divorced, Lisa would only get a quarter. But it worked both ways. If Lisa died, Hunter Thornton would get half of the lodge. The elder Seymours had to sign off on that. And if the couple divorced, Hunter would still get half of the lodge."

"Okay. Hunter Thornton was protecting his wealth from a potential gold-digger."

"There was also a life insurance policy on Hunter Thornton, two million dollars, with Lisa Thornton as the beneficiary. There was a similar one on Lisa."

"So, when Hunter died, Lisa should have received a couple of million dollars."

"Right. But what Lisa and the Seymours didn't know was that Hunter Thornton was, well, not very good at handling money. He was deeply in debt. In fact, I suspect that one of the reasons he married Lisa was so that he could stay in Canada and avoid his creditors."

"I see."

"Further, the prenuptial agreement was worded in such a way that Lisa would not only receive half of Hunter Thornton's assets but she would also be responsible for half of his debts. Lisa received the two-million-dollar insurance payout, but when Hunter's estate was settled, the debts not only consumed the entire life insurance payout, but Lisa and the Seymours were on the hook for an additional hundred and fifty thousand dollars. They used their line of credit to settle the estate, but, with the declining revenues at the lodge, they have never been able to pay it off."

"I suspect that this contributed to Lisa Thornton's distrust of lawyers and legal agreements?"

"I suspect so," Simmons agreed.

"Thank you for this," Wesson said. "Is there anything else that you can tell me?"

"No," Simmons said. "I think I have told you quite enough."

*****

"What did Lloyd Simmons tell you?" Edwards asked when Wesson returned.

Wesson told him and then asked, "Did you find anything else in the documents the trustee sent?"

"Still reading," Edwards answered. "But there was one interesting thing. You asked him to research the history of ownership of the lodge."

"Yes," Wesson answered. "You mean he actually did it?"

"Yes, he did. There is a summary here someplace." Edwards started leafing through papers.

"What's the gist of it?"

"The Seymours have owned the lodge for a long time, but they didn't actually build it."

"Who did?"

"A man named Donald Battenfield."

"Battenfield?"

"Yes," Edwards said. "Are you going to go back and talk to Lloyd Simmons about that?"

"No, I think I will go and talk to Travis Battenfield."

"Let me guess," Edwards said. "I can stay here and keep reading?"

"Right."

*****

Travis Battenfield's office was an unassuming brick storefront on Main Street. There were large display windows backed up by a grid of black steel bars. Wesson pushed through the front door and walked toward the single, cluttered desk directly ahead. A dumpy, middle-aged woman in a frilly blouse looked up.

"I'm here to see Travis Battenfield," Wesson said.

"Is he expecting you?"

"I hope not," Wesson answered.

"And which policeman are you?"

"Sergeant Wesson."

78

She picked up the phone and informed the lawyer who was there. As soon as she had hung up, a wooden door on the side of the reception area opened, and Battenfield walked out. He was dressed in blue jeans and a different plaid shirt.

"Great grillwork," Wesson said. "I assume it's there to protect you from your clients?"

"No, from police raids."

Battenfield led Wesson into his office. There was a battered oak desk piled high with files. The bookshelf behind the desk was crammed with law books, in no discernible order. A row of battered file cabinets filled an entire side wall.

"Are you here to make more unfounded allegations against my client?" Battenfield asked when he was seated in the swivel oak chair behind his desk.

"No, no, no," Wesson said as he settled into one of the thin, uncomfortable chairs across from the desk. "I'm here to make unfounded allegations against you."

Battenfield smiled. "Maybe it's time to get serious."

"I am serious," Wesson said. "As you know, we have been looking into a series of deaths of the owners of Moose Mountain Lodge. Years ago, your client, Billy Timmishin, knew the three people who have died recently, and that is why we have been asking him for background information. As we looked into the background of the Seymour family and the lodge, what do you think we found?"

"I have no idea," Battenfield answered. "You're the one with the vivid imagination."

"I thought we were going to be serious."

"Battenfield shrugged. "Sorry." But he didn't look sorry.

"We discovered that the lodge was not built by the Seymours but by a man named Donald Battenfield. Is that your father?"

"Grandfather."

"Can you tell me how the ownership passed to the Seymour family?"

"Is that relevant to what happened recently?"

"I have been drumming into my staff," Wesson said, "that if you want to understand what is happening in the present, it is helpful to know what happened in the past."

Battenfield shrugged. "It's a long and painful story, a tragedy, in the Shakespearean sense."

"I don't mind listening to long stories. It's a big part of my job."

"Since you don't know the story of how the lodge passed from my family to the Seymour family," Battenfield said, "I could tell you anything, and you'd never know whether it was true."

Wesson smiled. "We'll check. We always do. Verifying long stories is also a big part of our job."

Battenfield took a deep breath. "My grandfather, Donald Battenfield, had a vision to build a first-class hunting lodge in this area. Local government supported the idea. The federal government thought it was a good idea. It would create jobs for local people, including some of the First Nations, and bring in tourists who would spend money. He was allowed to pre-empt crown land, essentially homestead it, which means he had to make improvements. And he did. He had the lodge built and started building some of the cabins. They used local logs. There was a small, old sawmill on site. My grandfather was right. The lodge was successful and was attracting more and more hunters and fishers every year."

"Sounds good."

"My grandfather ran the lodge for about twenty years. Then, one summer, he hired John Seymour to work at the lodge. Seymour was a young man, about twenty, but he was bright, ambitious, and eager. He worked with enthusiasm and also seemed anxious to learn as much as he could about the running of the lodge."

"Okay."

"Seymour was laid off after hunting season in the fall. A couple of months later, he suddenly launched a lawsuit claiming ownership of the lodge. He hired a sharp lawyer."

"Lloyd Simmons."

"Actually, Lloyd's father, Delbert. At first, my grandfather thought the lawsuit was a joke. He didn't take it seriously."

"What was the basis of the claim? You can't just claim somebody's property and expect to win."

"I was getting to that. About fifty years earlier, John Seymour's grandfather had acquired the logging rights on that piece of crown land. He had logged it for about ten years and then shut down the operation. The old sawmill on the property had been his. Apparently, in the old logging regulations, there was a clause that said that if enough improvements were made on the land, say, if a town was built for the workers, the holder of the logging rights could claim the land under homestead legislation."

"But Seymour's grandfather hadn't done that?"

"No, but the regulations were badly drafted. They didn't define who had to make the improvements, as long as improvements were made. I expect the laws were deliberately vague in order to protect the logging companies. If the company provided the logs and lumber so its workers could build their own cabins, the land would still belong to the company, not the workers. The intent was to enable the company to keep logging the land rather than having the workers claim it as homesteads."

"So, Seymour claimed that the improvements your grandfather had made in building the lodge actually established *his* grandfather's logging homestead claim?"

"Seymour's lawyer did. My grandfather still thought the whole thing was a joke. He eventually hired a lawyer at the last minute, an unimaginative hack, but it was too late. He lost the case."

"That must have been pretty hard to take."

"It was. I'm not sure my grandfather ever recovered. He died when I was still quite young. I hadn't been born yet when they lost the lodge, but my grandfather had already brought my father into the business, so he could take it over when my grandfather died or retired. They all moved back to town. My grandfather had borrowed some of the money to build the lodge on his personal credit, so he was left with debt and no business to generate money to pay it off. Things were very lean for us when I was growing up."

"So, you had a grudge against the Seymour family. Is that why you took the case defending Billy Timmishin?"

"No, that was just the luck of the draw. There aren't a lot of lawyers in town, and we're all required to take a certain number of legal aid cases on a rotating basis. That case just happened to fall to me, but I can't say I was sorry about it either. If Billy had shot John Seymour, I probably would have waived my fee and defended him for free, or maybe even given him a medal, but I didn't particularly have anything against Hunter Thornton. I'd never met the man."

"You're still angry with the Seymour family? Did you kill John and Annemarie?"

"Battenfield laughed. "I wondered when you'd get around to thinking that. You know, time has a way of giving us a broader perspective. As the years went by, I came around to the idea that John Seymour, conniving bastard that he was, might have done us a favor. Losing the lodge forced us to move into town, and, poor as we were, that opened up a lot of new possibilities. The other thing it showed us was the importance of having a good lawyer. That's one of the reasons I went to law school. I can tell you I have had a much better life down here in town and made a lot more money as a lawyer than John Seymour ever made running that God-forsaken lodge up there in the middle of the wilderness."

Wesson thought about that. He stood up to go. "Thanks for your long story. It was very enlightening."

Battenfield also stood up. "If you are asking questions about me, does that mean you've given up on trying to charge Billy Timmishin with anything?"

Wesson paused. "I probably shouldn't tell you this, but no, I can't see me ever charging Billy with anything related to these recent deaths. It was always a long shot anyway. There was never really any clear evidence against him. I just wish he'd been willing to talk more."

"Don't we all?" Battenfield said.

Wesson had reached the door of the office, but Battenfield called him back. "Sergeant, could you come back in here for a moment?"

When Wesson had returned to his chair and Battenfield had also resumed sitting, the lawyer said, "I have debated for a while about showing you this. I have found that it is not always wise or safe to trust policemen with certain information. You can never tell what they might do with it."

"I'm not sure what you're talking about," Wesson said, intrigued.

The lawyer shuffled through some files in the clutter on his desk, found the one he wanted, opened it up, and pulled out a single sheet of typewritten paper. He hesitated and then handed the paper over to Wesson. The sergeant took it and began reading:

> *It was mid-morning, I had taken some hunters out to spend the day hunting, and I had gone into the equipment room to return a couple of rifles and some other equipment the hunters had decided at the last minute not to take with them. Just after I went in, I heard a shot coming from inside the building. I opened the other door and went into the office. John and Annemarie Seymour were there. The three of us ran across the office to the door on the other side, leading to the Thorntons' room. Mr. Seymour opened the door and went in first. Hunter Thornton was lying on the floor beside the bed. Lisa Thornton was standing by the door with her rifle in her hands. We all stood there for a moment in shock. Then, Mr. Seymour took the rifle out of Lisa's hands. He took the pillowcase off one of the pillows and wiped the rifle down. Then he handed the rifle to me. He said, "I will call the police. Billy, please take this rifle down to the front entrance and wait for the police there. When they get here, stop them there and give*

them the rifle." I waited down by the entrance for about an hour. When the police arrived, I walked toward them. They got out of the car, pulled out their guns, and crouched down behind the open car doors. I didn't understand what was happening. I thought Mr. Seymour would have told the police that I was bringing them the gun. I got closer and held out the gun to one of the policemen. Suddenly, the other one grabbed me from behind. They slammed me against the side of the car, searched me, handcuffed me, and put me into the back of the police car. I still didn't understand what was happening. They later took me to the police station. They put me into a little room and handcuffed me to a table. Later, two policemen came and began asking me questions. I answered at first, but then I realized that they thought I was the one who had shot Mr. Thornton. I was surprised, and I didn't understand what was happening. I stopped answering their questions and just stayed quiet.

Wesson read it over a second time. "Did Billy write this?" he asked. "It doesn't sound like him."

"I wrote it," Battenfield said.

"Did Billy dictate it?" Wesson started to ask and then amended. "Did Billy tell all this to you?"

Battenfield sighed. "As you may have gathered, Billy doesn't talk very much. He didn't know me and didn't really trust me. He dropped a couple of hints, and eventually, as he got to know me more, I pried a little more out of him and kind of filled in the blanks. He was pretty suspicious of white people and the legal system by then. It took a few months."

"So, it's not really his words, and he didn't sign it. It's mostly speculation on your part. Do you believe it?"

"I think something like that probably happened."

"Probably?" Wesson thought a moment. "I think it's just wishful thinking on your part. If you really thought this is what happened, why didn't you present it in court as a defense?"

Battenfield tilted his head. "My job is to get the best possible result for my client. By the time I had figured this out, the plea deal was already in place, and I figured it was about as good a result as Billy was likely to get. There was no proof, just the testimony of those involved, and it was three to one. Worse than that. Three respectable white people against one Native kid. Who would have believed Billy? Besides, you've talked to Billy. Can you imagine what he would be like on the stand? The prosecutor would have crushed him."

"So, you allowed Billy to go to jail."

"An older lawyer once told me that it doesn't matter what the truth is, only what you can prove in court."

"An older lawyer?"

"Lloyd Simmons."

Wesson nodded. He stood up to go. "Thanks for this. Can I keep it?"

"Sure," Battenfield said. "It's a copy. What are you going to do with it?"

Wesson shrugged. "Nothing. It's evidence for a case that was decided long ago. Not much I can do."

*****

"What do you think of this?" Edwards asked when Wesson had showed him the statement.

"It's absolutely worthless from a legal point of view," Wesson answered. "As evidence, it is merely suggestive."

"In what sense?"

"Rick Tessam said Billy was 'compliant.' I didn't necessarily buy it. And when I asked Billy what he did for the Seymours, he said something about always doing exactly what Mr. Seymour told him to do."

"It fits."

"Yes, but only if that is really what Billy's character is." Wesson paused. "Did you find anything else in all that paperwork the trustee sent over?"

"A lot of dreary reading," Edwards answered. "But there was one interesting thing."

"What's that?"

"Remember that the lawyer, Lloyd Simmons, said there were matching two-million-dollar life insurance policies on the Thorntons?"

"Yes."

"Well, apparently Lisa Thornton continued paying into hers for a bit after Hunter died and then converted it to a paid-up policy. It's not worth two million dollars but enough to clear the line of credit."

"I don't know who that's going to benefit, other than the bank," Wesson said. "Anything else?"

"Yes, something came in from tech support."

"What's that?"

"They bypassed the password and opened Annemarie Seymour's phone."

"And?"

"As you know, the Seymours never used their cell phones much. Annemarie made very few calls, only a couple between the time John Seymour died and the time she died, and those were made to the phone at the lodge."

"So?"

"But she did receive a series of text messages. The techies gave us a transcript." Edwards handed over a sheet of paper. It read:

> *April 27: Are you there?*
> *April 29: I love you. I miss you very much.*
> *May 1: I am safe on the other side.*
> *May 3: Don't worry about me. I am at peace.*
> *May 5: It's wonderful here. Come and join me.*
> *May 7: We have two sons and a daughter here*
> *   waiting to meet you. They miss you.*
> *May 8: It's time.*
> *May 9: Come tonight.*

"Fascinating," Wesson said. "The last one was sent in the evening just before Annemarie committed suicide."

"Someone was pushing her to do it."

"Who sent the texts?" Wesson asked.

"They were sent from John Seymour's cell phone."

"The one we haven't been able to find."

"Right."

"So who sent the messages?" Wesson asked. "Any theories?"

"No good ones. You're the one with more experience. What do you think?"

"The obvious explanation is that the phone was buried with John Seymour. Annemarie believed in communing with the dead, remember, so she just might have done that."

"And John texted her from the grave? You really think that's what happened?"

"No," Wesson said.

"Then who?"

"That's the question, isn't it? Who would have had access to John Seymour's phone?"

"Maybe anybody. I guess he could have lost it or it was stolen."

"Maybe, but I don't think so," Wesson said. "It had to be somebody at the lodge or somebody who went there."

"But nobody went there, except you, I guess, and the doctor."

"Lisa Thornton could have done it, but why would she?"

"To get rid of her mother so she would inherit the lodge?" Edwards suggested.

"Why bother? Annemarie was older and not in great health. She was likely going to die soon anyway. Lisa could have waited."

"Unless there was some reason to speed up the process. Maybe someone was offering to buy the lodge and her mother didn't want to sell."

"Did the trustee come across anything like that?" Wesson asked.

"No."

"It's a puzzle."

"It could have been that Indian caretaker," Edwards suggested.

"George Tessam?"

"Sure. He could have had access."

"Yes, but why would he? What would he have to gain? Where's the motive?"

Edwards shrugged. "Beats me."

The two men sat in silence for a while.

"Unless it's the final clue," Wesson said.

"The final clue to what?"

"I'm not sure yet. I'm going to think on it overnight."

Tuesday, June 12

Wesson rang the doorbell, and again, after a flurry of noise and a few moments of silence, the door was opened by Bob Hawthorne.

Hawthorne looked Wesson over and then said, "You're back? You've got to stop coming here. You're going to make the neighbors think there are criminals living here."

"There *are* criminals living here."

"Sure, but there are criminals living behind the doors of a lot of our neighbors' houses too, and you're not hassling them."

Wesson smiled. "That's probably true, but we haven't caught them yet." When Hawthorne said nothing more, Wesson said, "This is probably the last time. For a while at least. I want to talk to Billy Timmishin."

"What? Again? You don't have any brick walls back at the station to talk to?" Hawthorne smiled. "At least he's here this time."

When Billy arrived at the front door, Wesson said, "Billy, this is not an interrogation. I am not going to ask you any questions. I just want to talk to you, man to man. Unofficially. No interrogation rooms. No tape recorders. No lawyers. We can talk anywhere you like, here, on the front porch, in the backyard, in a park, going for a walk down the street. I don't care. Your choice. I'll do the talking, and you can just listen."

Billy was silent for a moment looking at Wesson. Then he said, "I want my lawyer."

Hawthorne, standing beside Billy, shrugged.

"Okay, Billy," Wesson said. "If that's the way you want it." He sighed. "Let's go somewhere else."

Wesson signaled to Edwards waiting in the car, and Edwards dialed a cell phone. The call was over when Wesson and Billy reached the car. They got in and drove a short distance to Main Street.

*****

"We have an appointment to see Mr. Battenfield," Wesson said to the middle-aged receptionist.

The lawyer came out of his office, opened another door, and led them into a different room. This one was furnished with comfortable chairs around a round table. The room was painted a pleasant blue, and there was a small kitchenette in the corner.

"Coffee?" Battenfield asked.

Billy shook his head, but Wesson said, "Yes, please. I'd like one. This might take a little while."

When Battenfield had poured four coffees and they were seated around the table, Wesson began.

"Billy, I wanted to just talk to you informally," Wesson said. "As I explained, you don't have to say anything. I want to tell you a story."

The others said nothing, and Wesson continued.

"The story is about a young man named Billy. He lived with his mother in a small house. Billy lived a quiet life and never got into trouble. He did what he was supposed to do and never demanded very much of life."

If Billy was surprised by Wesson's approach, he gave no sign, but the lawyer raised his eyebrows quizzically.

Wesson continued. "On the day Billy finished high school, his mother died unexpectedly."

Billy winced very slightly.

"Billy didn't know what to do, but his mother had told him that if he ever needed help, he should go up to the Moose Mountain Lodge and apply for a job. And that is what he did. Billy worked there for about a year, doing whatever needed doing. He was a good employee because he did what he had always done—he did what he was told. One day, he was in the equipment room putting things away when he heard a shot. Billy, following the noise, went into the next room, which was the office, where his employers, John and Annemarie, were. All three of them went on to the next room, where his employers' daughter, Lisa, was standing, holding a rifle. Her husband was lying dead on the floor. John took a pillowcase, wiped off the rifle, and handed it to Billy. He told Billy to take the rifle down to the front entrance to the lodge grounds and give it to the police when they arrived. Billy did what he had always done—he did what he was told. He took the rifle and went down to the entrance to wait for the police. When the police arrived, Billy walked toward the police officers to give them the rifle. Billy thought that his employers would have told the police the truth, but in fact his employers must have told the police that Billy had shot their son-in-law. The police pointed their guns at Billy as if he was a criminal. There was a very good chance that the police might have shot Billy. In fact, that was probably what his employers wanted to happen. Billy was not shot, but the outcome was almost as bad. Billy's employers and their daughter all told the police that Billy had done the shooting. Billy was arrested, handcuffed, put into a police car, and driven to the police station, where he was interrogated. Billy at first tried to explain, but then he realized it was hopeless, and he just stopped talking. That was when Billy stopped trusting people and stopped doing what he was told to do."

Through all of this recitation, Wesson was watching Billy like a hawk. Billy was staring at him intently but did not change his facial expression. Wesson stole a glance at Battenfield, but the lawyer appeared equally stone-faced, almost holding his breath to hear what Wesson would say next.

Wesson continued. "Billy was given a lawyer, whom he didn't trust any more than the police at first. But the lawyer promised to help him as much as he could, and eventually Billy trusted the lawyer enough that he agreed to plead guilty to second degree murder. Billy was sentenced to prison, where even more wicked and unspeakably terrible things happened to him."

Wesson paused to sip his coffee. "After a very long time, thirteen years, something good finally happened. Billy's lawyer told him that he was being released to live in a halfway house. After a while, Billy was told that if he stayed out of trouble and lived in the halfway house for a few months, he would not go back to prison but would be released."

Wesson again watched Billy, but the young man still showed no emotion. If anything, he seemed slightly more relaxed.

"But Billy was no longer willing to do as he was told," Wesson continued. "He had learned things in prison, and he had changed. Billy was determined to get revenge on his employers. He decided to kill them."

Finally, there was a reaction. Billy's lip twitched, and he leaned forward slightly.

"One Sunday night, Billy crawled out through the window of his room. He went down the street and found a pickup truck. It is possible that Billy had seen the owner get out of the truck, leave it unlocked, and put the key under the floor mat the previous afternoon when Billy and some of the other residents of the halfway house had gone for a walk. Or maybe Billy just got lucky and found an unlocked truck with the keys inside. Billy started the truck and drove up to Moose Mountain Lodge. Billy told me that he had never had a driver's license, and that may be true. However, Billy also said that he did whatever his employer told him to do, and that included driving clients out to the woods to hunt and driving clients out to rivers and lakes where they could fish. Anyway, when Billy got to the lodge, he broke into the equipment room and selected a rifle. My guess is that it was a Remington

3600, Lisa's rifle, the rifle she had used to shoot her husband. It would have seemed an appropriate and just choice to Billy. I have wondered how Billy could see in the darkened lodge. Maybe his employers left night-lights on. Or maybe Billy also took some night vision goggles from the equipment room. I saw some there when I was investigating a burglary at the lodge. Anyway, armed with the rifle, Billy went through the office to what had been Lisa and Hunter Thornton's room. I think he planned to kill Lisa first and then go upstairs and kill her parents. But when he went into the room, he was surprised to find her father, John Seymour, there. It must have been quite a shock when John woke up and saw Billy threatening him with a gun. It induced a heart attack. John tried to get out of bed, perhaps to get his medication, but he fell to the floor. He might have tried to grab his cell phone to call for help, but Billy took that away from him and put it into his pocket. And then Billy watched as John lay on the floor and died from the heart attack. It probably surprised him that John had died so easily without being shot. But Billy was still resolved to kill the rest of the family."

There was still no reaction from Billy or the lawyer.

Wesson continued. "Next, Billy went upstairs. He went into his employer's wife's bedroom. He approached the bed to kill her, but I suspect he saw something on the bedside table. It was a pill bottle containing a drug called Xanifol. Billy recognized it because it was the drug his mother had used to commit suicide years earlier. Billy picked up the bottle and was holding it in his hand. Either before or after this, Billy also saw on the table a book called *Talking with the Dead: Communicating with Your Dearly Departed Made Easy.* Perhaps he also saw some books with similar titles on her bookshelf. Billy was intelligent, a good student, and the presence of these books would tell him that Annemarie likely believed in communicating with the dead. At some point, Annemarie partially woke up. Only partially because it was the middle of the night and she was likely still under the influence of the Xanifol, which would have helped her sleep. But she saw Billy standing beside the bed, holding the rifle and the bottle of pills. In her muddled state, she thought Billy was her husband, and she called out in her sleep, 'John.' As I said, Billy was far more intelligent than most people ever gave him credit for, and he quickly realized that there was a better way to kill Annemarie than to shoot her. He put the Xanifol down and quietly left the room. As Billy was leaving, he must also have looked around the office and Lisa's bedroom and seen all of the empty liquor bottles. It was an easy conclusion that Lisa would drink herself into a stupor most nights, and that suggested a way to kill her. Billy put the rifle, and the goggles if he had them, back into the equipment room and left the lodge. Billy then drove the truck back to town, parked it on Main Street, crawled back through the window of his bedroom, and caught some sleep before morning. Oh, and it can be taken for granted that Billy was smart enough to wear gloves so he wouldn't leave fingerprints."

Wesson paused to take another sip of coffee, then continued.

"Billy waited a few days, no suspicion fell on him, and he realized he was in the clear. So, he put the next stage of his plan into action. He had kept the cell phone that he had taken from John. Now he turned it on and began sending text messages to Annemarie, hoping that, with her belief in communicating with the dead, she would think they were messages coming from John from beyond the grave. 'Are you there?' he wrote. Then a couple of days later: 'I love you. I miss you very much.' And again: 'I am safe on the other side. Don't worry about me. I'm at peace. It's wonderful here.' And then the messages intensified, a new one every evening: 'We have two sons and a daughter here waiting for you. It's time. Come tonight.' That last one was sent on the evening of May 9, and that night Annemarie did what the messages told her to do. She took an overdose of Xanifol, committing suicide."

Wesson paused. "It must have been quite an exhilarating experience for Billy, to realize that he was now giving the orders and other people were doing what he told them to do. After that, Lisa Thornton was easy. Once Billy had learned that Annemarie was dead, he waited a few days. Then, late on the evening of Sunday, May 27, he took out John's phone again. This time he phoned the lodge. Maybe he had phoned Lisa's cell phone and got no answer. Anyway, Lisa answered the lodge phone. The lodge phone had call display, so I am guessing that Lisa realized it was someone using John's cell phone. Or maybe she was too drunk to look at the caller's identity. There is no evidence that Lisa believed in talking to the dead, so Billy took a different approach with her. There is a record of the phone call, but I don't know exactly what was said. I suspect it went something like this. I think Billy told her who he was. Maybe he said that he knew she had killed her husband and that she and her parents had blamed it on him. Likely he said that he was out for revenge. I am pretty sure that Billy said he had killed Lisa's father and mother and now he was coming to kill her. He probably told her that he was already close to the lodge, in range of the cell tower up there, so there was no use phoning the police for help. They were at least an hour away. By the time the police got there, Billy would already have killed her. Everything worked out just the way Billy had planned. Lisa had probably concluded that George Tessam was not likely to help her. She grabbed her rifle and began driving down the mountain road into town. As Billy expected, she was already drunk. She missed a turn in the road, rolled down an embankment, and was killed, just another drunk driving accident. I don't know how Billy found out that Lisa was dead. Maybe Rick Tessam told him, or maybe he didn't know until I came to interview him and told him. Anyway, once Billy knew she was dead, he smashed the cell phone and threw it in a dumpster or the river, somewhere where we will never find it."

Wesson stopped talking and looked at Billy. There was absolute silence in the room. Billy's face showed nothing. Finally, Wesson said, "Thanks for listening, Billy. What do you think of my story?"

Billy showed no emotion whatsoever. He remained stone-faced and silent. Wesson became convinced that Billy would not say any more this time than he had any other time. But then Billy took a deep breath and broke his silence.

"You have told me an interesting story," Billy said. "Now I will tell you one." He paused. "This land used to be protected by a great wall. One day, Old Woman said, 'I want to climb up onto the wall and see the great world beyond.' But Raven said, 'Do not do that. If you climb onto the wall, it will collapse, and disaster will come.' The next day, Old Woman said again, 'I want to climb up onto the wall and see the great world beyond.' But Eagle said, 'Do not do that. If you climb onto the wall, it will collapse, and disaster will come.' The third day, Old Woman said, 'I want to climb up onto the wall and see the great world beyond.' But no one said anything. There was silence. So, Old Woman climbed up onto the wall. She cried out, 'Little Man, come up here and see the great world beyond the wall.' So, Little Man climbed up onto the wall, and together they looked at the great world beyond the wall. Then, when they had seen enough, they climbed back down. The next day, when they awakened in the morning, Old Woman said, 'Raven was wrong. The great wall is still there, and no disaster has come.' The second day, when they awakened in the morning, Old Woman said, 'Eagle was wrong. The great wall is still there, and no disaster has come.' On the third day, when Old Woman and Little Man awakened in the morning, they looked, and the great wall was gone. In the inlet was a large ship. The white man had come." Billy stopped, and then he smiled and said, "Like what you told me, that is an interesting story, but there is no evidence to prove whether or not it is true."

Wesson nodded and said, "There may be no evidence, but you and I both know the story is true."

"Which story?" Billy said. "The one about Old Woman and Little Man?"

"No, the other one."

Billy smiled. "You could never prove it. What are you going to do, send me to prison without evidence like your white man's court did last time?"

Wesson did not smile. No one spoke for a full minute.

"Can I go now?" Billy asked.

"Yes, Billy, you can go now," Wesson answered.

Travis Battenfield cleared his throat. "Sergeant, before you go, could I talk to you about another matter?"

"Sure," Wesson answered. "Edwards, why don't you drive Mr. Timmishin home and then come back and get me?"

Battenfield led Wesson back into his cluttered office.

"That was an interesting story," the lawyer said. "Do you believe it?"

"Yes, I think that's what happened."

"What were you expecting from telling it to Billy?"

"I was hoping for a reaction, to confirm it," Wesson said. "And I think I got that. That was the longest response I have ever heard from Billy."

"That's for sure, but Billy never said that you were right."

"I think Billy managed to indicate that I was right without actually saying it."

"So, what are you going to do about it?"

Wesson shrugged. "Probably nothing. Billy's right. I don't have any evidence."

"It doesn't matter what the truth is, only what you can prove in court."

"If you say so," Wesson answered. "Is that what you wanted to talk to me about?"

"No," Battenfield answered.

The lawyer opened a file on his desk, removed a sheet of paper, and handed it to Wesson.

"What's this?" the policeman asked. "A confession?"

Battenfield smiled. "No. You had an autopsy performed on John Seymour, right?"

"Yes."

"So, the police lab would still have tissue samples?"

"Probably."

"That is a court order requesting a tissue sample from John Seymour."

"For what purpose?"

"DNA testing." The lawyer smiled. "You are a better interrogator than you know, Sergeant. You elicited a piece of information from Billy that I didn't have before. You remember the second time you interrogated Billy?"

"Interviewed, not interrogated."

"It felt like an interrogation," the lawyer said. "Anyway, Billy said that his mother told him if he ever needed help, he should go to the lodge and ask for a job."

"He also said that in the first interview."

"Yes, but he added something new, that his mother had worked at the lodge for a time when she was young."

Wesson thought that over. "A paternity test?" he asked. "That's a long shot."

"Not necessarily. There was never any indication of who Billy's father was. It was assumed it was somebody on the reserve, but why didn't the father come forward, and why didn't Billy's mother say who it was or ask for child support? But if she got pregnant at the lodge…It would explain why she stopped working there."

"John Seymour wouldn't likely have agreed to a paternity test back then," Wesson mused.

"It would have been her word against his," the lawyer said. "And she would not have been believed any more than Billy's story that he hadn't shot Hunter Thornton would have been believed."

"John Seymour was a bit of a bastard, and Annemarie had a number of miscarriages," Wesson said. "It's possible, I suppose, but I still think it's unlikely."

"No more than that cock and bull story you just told Billy."

*****

"Did you get Mr. Timmishin safely back to his halfway house?" Wesson asked.

"Yes."

"Did he say anything?"

"Not a word."

"There's a surprise."

Edwards was silent for a moment. "Do you really think Lisa Thornton killed her husband?"

"Yes. It's the theory that best fits the facts."

"But why?"

"We'll probably never know now, especially with them all being dead. I don't think it was planned. Maybe shock or disappointment. She must eventually have figured out that her husband didn't have money and they weren't moving to New York."

Edwards nodded. "New husband. American. He was practically begging to be shot."

"Edwards!"

"What?"

"You're developing a sense of humor."

"Is that permitted?"

"Yes, but it's totally unexpected."

Friday, June 29

Edwards was standing in the door of Wesson's office. Wesson looked up.

"Yes?"

"I was just wondering what happened with those files we were working on...you know, the ones about what happened up at the lodge."

"I closed them."

"What?"

"I closed them."

"All of them?"

"Yes. John Seymour died of a heart attack, Annemarie Seymour committed suicide, and Lisa Thornton died in a drunk driving accident."

"That's all technically true," Edwards protested, "but it's not what happened."

"Cases don't always turn out the way you want them to," Wesson said. "You need to learn that."

"But it's ironic, isn't it?"

"You mean that the only murder we could convict Billy of was the one he didn't commit?"

"Yeah, it doesn't seem right."

"Human justice is imperfect, Edwards. But sometimes the result is something close to fair, and that is all you can ask for."

"Was this fair?"

"Not bad in the end," Wesson said. "If we had the evidence to convict him, what could we have charged Billy with? In John Seymour's death, what? Failure to provide the necessities of life? Uttering threats? At a stretch, manslaughter? And what could we charge him with regarding Annemarie's death? Bullying on social media? Counseling to commit suicide? Now that assisted suicide is legal, good luck making that stick. The same with Lisa's death. Maybe uttering threats, but he didn't force her to get into her SUV and drive drunk. Add all of those up, and what kind of sentence would Billy likely have been given? Thirteen years maybe, at the most?"

"Well…"

"And consider Lisa Thornton and the Seymours. Lisa murdered her husband in cold blood, then conspired with her parents to send an innocent man to prison and ruin his life. They're all dead now. Capital punishment sounds about right to me."

"So, the official results are wrong but the sentences are right?"

"That's the way it looks to me. In a sense, justice was done," Wesson said. "And remember that the Seymours used a legal technicality to steal the lodge from the Battenfield family? The land is reverting to one of its original owners."

"Travis Battenfield?"

"No, Billy Timmishin, a member of the First Nations group who originally owned the land. The paternity test came back positive."

"But will Billy be able to run the lodge?" Edwards asked.

"I think Billy picks up more than he seems to. Remember those text messages to Annemarie? One mentioned that she had three children waiting for her. Billy somehow picked up that she had had several miscarriages. He was working all the time in the equipment room next to the office. The family probably talked freely while he was in earshot, thinking no more about it than if he was the family dog."

"I guess."

"Billy helped with most aspects of the operation, including dealing with clients. And I suspect his friends, the Tessams, will help him."

"You were right," Edwards said. "If we want to understand what is happening in the present, we need to find out what happened in the past. This has been a learning experience."

"Speaking of the present, aren't you supposed to be on traffic patrol?"

Without a word, Edwards turned and left the office.

The Honeymoon

"We're on our honeymoon!" Miranda gushed. She had an infectious way of talking that sounding like a brook babbling over a stony bed. "When we saw the sign offering trail rides, we knew we had to come in."

"You're lucky," the man called Lofty answered. "We offer rides ranging from a couple of hours to a week, but we're closing down for the winter in a couple of days."

"Wonderful!" she said, "We'll ride for at least three or four hours."

"Have you ridden before?" Lofty asked.

"Oh, yes, we've both ridden," she answered, "but never on a trail ride in the mountains."

"Slim!" Lofty called to a tall, gangly young man coming out of the doorway of one of the barns. "Saddle up the bay and the mare for a trail ride."

Miranda and Walter had driven their gray Honda up the long lane past the ranch house and parked it among a group of barns.

"Your honeymoon?" Lofty asked. "People usually plan their honeymoons in advance and make reservations."

"But that's the point!" Miranda burbled. "Marriage is the greatest adventure of all. It's a journey, and you never know where it's going to take you. So, it doesn't make any sense to spend our honeymoon doing something predictable. We made reservations for the first night, and then we just went out on the road. We're going wherever we feel like going for two weeks."

"Well, you might think about leaving those backpacks behind in your car. Bouncing up and down on a horse, the straps are going to start cutting into your shoulders after a while."

Walter spoke for the first time, in a voice that was much more measured and controlled than his wife's. "We packed everything we'll need for any adventure in these backpacks," he said. "They've got padded straps, and we've ridden with them before. We'll keep them."

"Suit yourself." Lofty shrugged. "There's a line shack a couple of hours out along the trail by a lake. There and back would be a good ride. I'll give you a good deal, a hundred dollars each."

"Sounds great!" Miranda enthused. "Pay the man, Walter."

Walter was of medium height, while Miranda was tall for a woman, maybe an inch or so taller. Walter reached into his pocket, pulled out a roll of bills and counted out ten twenties.

"Thanks," Lofty said. "I'll have a receipt waiting for you when you get back."

There wasn't much more that could be said, so Miranda and Walter wandered around enjoying the scenery and looking into the doorway of the only barn that was open. After a few minutes, the lanky ranch hand came out of one of the barns leading three horses.

"Howdy, folks," he said, coming toward Miranda and Walter. Looking at Walter, he presented the reins of the bay horse. "This here is Rocky." Turning toward Miranda, he offered another set of reins. "And this is Molly."

Miranda's short, black hair flipped as she spoke. "Molly? That doesn't sound like a very exciting animal to ride when I'm going on an adventure!"

"Now, don't go selling Molly short." Lofty intervened. "Molly's a good trail horse. She's got good speed and power, but she's even-tempered. She'll serve you well."

Meanwhile, the youth named Slim had expertly swung up into the saddle of the third horse. With a little less grace but with no problems, Walter and Miranda mounted their horses as well.

"Take Walter and Miranda out to the line shack by the lake and then come back," Lofty instructed Slim. "They've paid for a four-hour ride."

His eyes suddenly turned away. A cloud of dust was moving up the gravel road toward the ranch. "I wonder who that is," he said softly. "Not likely to be more customers just stopping in on their way by."

Turning back, he said in a louder voice, "Get going, Slim. When you reach the ridge across the field, look back. If it is more customers, you can wait there, and I'll bring them to you."

Slim nodded. "Let's go," he said and turned his horse away from the ranch house. At a brisk walk, he led Miranda and Walter between two of the barns. There they picked up a trail that led through an open gate and then through a gap in a grove of trees toward a large hayfield. The trail veered off to the right around the hayfield, but the hay had recently been cut and baled, and the remaining grass was short. They cut across the field, angling somewhat to the right. Slim slowed his horse, allowing Miranda and Walter to come up beside him, one on each side.

"What did Lofty mean that that new vehicle was unlikely to bring more customers?" Miranda asked.

"You don't know?" Slim asked. "What were you doing on that road anyway?"

"It's our honeymoon," Miranda answered. "It's the start of the great adventure of our life together, so we decided to just go wherever the road takes us. What's wrong with that road?"

"Nothing's wrong with the road," Slim said, "except that it doesn't go anywhere. There used to be a town called Richer another ten or fifteen miles up the road, but the mine closed down a few years ago, and there was a small sawmill operation that closed last year. Richer is a ghost town now. Nobody lives there. This ranch is about the only thing on the road now, so nobody just passes by."

"Except us!" Miranda countered.

"Except you," Slim agreed.

"Is that why you are closing down the trail rides for the winter?"

"Yep," Slim answered. "They won't plow the road just for us in the winter, and we would be snowed in. So, the Major is moving the horses down to his other property on the highway."

"Who's the Major?"

"That's what we call the boss. Rick and Rita Major own this place. They sleep up at the ranch house. Lofty and me sleep in the bunkhouse."

"It must be hard to be so isolated."

"I kind of like it, but it does take a bit to get used to it. A couple of days ago, the cops were looking for a couple of men in a black SUV who had done an armed robbery at a bank or something. But we didn't hear about it on the radio or TV or the internet or a newspaper. There's no reception up here. We're largely cut off from the outside world. The Major was talking to another rancher on the phone, and he happened to mention the robbery. Otherwise, we wouldn't have known about it. And now the phone company says they won't maintain the line after this fall."

There were a couple of moments of silence before Miranda spoke. "Oh, I get it!" she burbled. "Is this one of those holdups you stage for the tourists?"

"Uh...no, we don't do that."

Miranda stared at Slim as if she didn't know if she believed him. Then she laughed, a sound that was pleasant and mysteriously alluring all at the same time.

They rode in silence for a bit. When they reached the end of the hayfield, they rejoined the trail. It led into some trees and then wound its way up a substantial rise. Walter happened to be on the left, and he took the lead. After a number of twists and turns, the trail opened up into an open area along the top of a ridge.

"Did you hear a shot?" Walter asked.

Slim and Miranda pulled up beside Walter, who was looking back toward the ranch house. They could see it clearly, but the trees on the slope below them would make their horses invisible to anyone looking up from below.

"What?" Slim asked.

"Did you hear a shot?" Walter repeated.

"Why'd you ask that?" Slim asked.

"Look," Walter responded.

Clearly visible beside the ranch house was a black SUV. In the space in front of the barns, a man dressed in dark clothing was standing, his right hand extended outward. In front of him, face down on the ground, was Lofty. He was not moving, and his hat was lying a few feet away from him.

"The bank robbers?" Miranda breathed.

"Looks like it," Walter answered.

"What can we do?" Miranda asked.

"Don't think there's anything we can do," Slim answered.

"Do you have a gun?" Walter asked him.

"Nope."

"But we're going on a trail ride," Miranda protested. "What if we met a bear or a mountain lion? How would you protect us?"

"We're not going that far," Slim said defensively. "On the longer rides, Lofty usually brings a rifle. But he never gave me one."

"That's...that's irresponsible," Miranda protested.

"Wouldn't make any difference," Slim said.

"Why not?" Miranda demanded.

"I wouldn't go back down there even if I had a gun. I wouldn't stand a chance against criminals. They've got a lot more experience using guns, and they've probably got better guns too," Slim said. "And that means that right now we should get off this ridge."

Miranda stared. "Why? Do you think they might come after us?"

"This is where we were supposed to look back to see if there were any more clients for the trail ride. If Lofty could see us, then they can too if they happen to look up here. Right now, those criminals have no reason to know we're here. We need to get off the ridge before they do."

They turned their horses away from the ranch house and dropped down the far side of the ridge.

"What are we going to do?" Miranda demanded.

"Don't think we have much choice," Slim answered.

"You mean we just have to hide out here in the woods until they leave?" she asked.

"Not much chance of that."

"Why?"

"This ranch is on a road to nowhere. If the robbers are looking for a place to hide out for a while, they've found it. They could stay there for months, and no one would find them."

"But I thought you said you were moving down to the highway in a few days," Miranda said. "Wouldn't someone notice if you don't show up?"

"No. It's just us moving from one of our properties to the other. Nobody else's involved."

"Then can we go to a neighbor?" Miranda asked.

"I told you there's no neighbors," Slim answered. "We're the only ones on this road."

"Then we need to get out of here," Miranda demanded.

"That's not going to be easy," Slim said. "Look around. This ranch is in a valley, mountains on both sides, and it narrows down there at the mouth of the valley. There's fences on the fields, so the only way out's down the lane past the barns and the ranch house, right past those guys."

"We'll wait for dark." Walter inserted himself into the discussion.

"Won't work," Slim said. "We might be able to sneak past, but not with the horses. The other horses would hear them and start making a racket. If we did get past, we' be out on the road on foot with no food and more than fifty miles from any help. Think you can walk fifty miles without food?"

"If we waited for dark and rode the horses up the lane as fast as they'll go, we might get past them before they saw us," Walter suggested.

"And then what?" Slim answered. "You think we could outrun an SUV for fifty miles in the dark? These horses are good, but they're not that good."

"Then what can we do?" Miranda wailed.

"Only one thing we can do," Slim said.

"What's that?" Miranda demanded.

"Did Lofty tell you we offer longer rides?" Slim asked.

"Yes," Miranda answered. "He said rides up to a week long."

"This ranch is in a valley. The valley winds back into the mountains for miles. Then a trail leads up over a pass and down into another valley on the other side. There's another ranch there, the Lazy C, owned by an old couple, Phil and Maggie Cooper. Takes about three days to get there, a week to go there and back. It's a long, hard ride. Think you can do it?"

"But what will we eat?" Miranda asked.

"There's some food and other supplies up at the line shack we're heading to. We'll be alright, as long as you can ride for that long."

Miranda looked at Walter and then turned back. "We can do it," she said.

Slim urged his horse forward along the trail. "You wanted an adventure," he said over his shoulder. "You're going to get it."

"I'm ready for an adventure," Miranda called to his back, "as long as Molly is!"

She kicked her horse forward until she had caught up and was riding beside Slim. Walter followed some distance behind. The trail went down a small slope and then opened out into another hayfield that was at least two or three times larger than the previous one.

"Do you still think Molly isn't a good enough horse for you?" Slim asked without looking at Miranda. "Has she given you any trouble?"

"Well, no," Miranda conceded. "She's more spirited than I expected." The truth was that Molly had proven to be quick and sure-footed, responsive to her rider, and perhaps more powerful than Walter's horse.

"Molly has been ridden over the pass several times without any trouble," Slim continued, this time looking directly at Miranda. "She's one of the best trail horses we have. Since I've been here, I've learned not to judge a horse's temperament and ability by its name."

"Never judge a book by its cover." Miranda nodded.

"I don't read books," Slim answered.

Miranda's endearing babbling brook laugh echoed across the field. "How long have you worked here?" she asked.

"About a year and a half. I was hired to help with the trail rides and the haying."

"Does that include this field? How do you get the equipment to cut the hay up the ridge?"

"Yeah. This field is part of the ranch. The ridge slope's not as steep farther down near the creek, and there's a lane between the two fields. We could've gone that way, but the trail we took is shorter and okay for horses."

Miranda smiled at him. "And how did you get the name Slim?"

The youth shrugged. "Lofty figured Slim sounded like a good cowboy name to use in front of the tourists. My real name's Trevor."

"Trevor!" Miranda laughed again. "Well, it's good to meet you, Trevor."

They rode the full length of the field and then entered the woods again. The trail was just wide enough for Slim and Miranda to ride side by side.

"Did the Major make this entire trail?" Miranda asked after a while.

"I doubt it," Slim answered. "It was probably an old Native trail, widened into a logging road. Farther up, above the tree line, it narrows again."

They rode on for well over an hour, the trail winding through the trees along the right side of the valley, sloping steadily upward. Finally, the trees began to thin, and they came out into a broad, flat area with a small lake in the center, surrounded by long stretches of grass and shrubs.

"Over there," Slim said. He led them toward a small shack on the right side of the lake along the edge of the trees. "The horses need to graze here for a bit. There's not much to eat farther up."

He slid effortlessly out of the saddle and began loosening the saddle straps on his horse. Miranda and Walter also dismounted, somewhat less gracefully. Walter moved over to show them how to loosen the saddle straps on their horses.

"Stiff?" Slim asked as they began moving around slowly, stretching their legs and their shoulders. "It's going to get a lot worse."

"A little," Miranda admitted.

"You got any food or warmer jackets in those backpacks?" Slim asked.

"No," Walter answered curtly.

"We're on our honeymoon," Miranda added as if in explanation.

Slim nodded and walked toward the shack. "You walk around and limber up," he said over his shoulder.

A couple of minutes later, he was back, carrying six canteens. "Up there through the trees," he said, pointing, "there's a little spring. Take these up there and fill them all. Have a drink while you're there."

The horses were grazing contentedly as Walter and Miranda set off for the spring. Slim headed back to the cabin.

It was a little longer walk than Walter and Miranda had expected, but they found the spring easily enough, following a springy channel though the grass. The water was bubbling out through a gap in the rocks at a place where the slope along the side of the valley became steeper.

When they got back, they saw that Slim had laid out a small pile in front of the shack. "We'll let the horses graze another half hour or so and then load up," he said.

Then it was Slim's turn to wander off into the woods in the direction of the spring. It was considerably over a half hour before he returned. Walter and Miranda had been looking at their watches.

"Not much use for those out here," Slim said. He walked over to where his horse was grazing, tightened the cinches, and led it back toward the cabin.

Walter and Miranda, gradually coming to the realization that they were going to be expected to do their share of the work, went off to get their horses. When they got back to the shack, Slim showed them how to cinch up the saddles again.

Then he brought over the canteens and two coils of rope for each horse and showed them how to fix them to straps hanging from the saddle by the saddle horn.

"What are the ropes for?" Miranda asked. "You're not expecting us to rope cattle, are you?"

"Rope's always handy," Slim answered.

Slim next handed them each a sleeping bag rolled up tightly and instructed them to tie the bags in a similar way behind their saddles. Behind his saddle, Slim tied another sleeping bag and an even bigger roll of some similar material. Then he handed them each a large canvas coat.

"You can just lay those over the saddle in front of you," he said. "But it'll be colder farther up, and you'll want to put them on then. I even found a couple of cowboy hats. I hope they fit."

He handed the hats over. Miranda's seemed a bit tight and Walter's a bit loose, but they would do. Finally, he handed each of them a set of bulging saddlebags to be placed astride the horses behind the saddle. Over his own horse, Slim slung a couple of white canvas bags.

"We're not too bad for food," Slim said. "Would have been more earlier in the year, but we'll be okay. There are cups and plates in your saddle bags, and some beef jerky, granola bars, and trail mix, nuts, and dried fruit. You can eat some as we ride. We won't be stopping again for a while. We've also got some canned beans, oatmeal, sugar, and coffee. Authentic cowboy food. Not a lot of variety, but it'll fill you up."

"Aren't you going to hunt along the way like a real cowboy?" Miranda asked teasingly.

"Nope. I'm not a hunter, just a hired hand. I already told you I don't have a gun."

"There wasn't one in the shack?" Walter asked.

"Nope," Slim answered. "Just this knife." He pointed to a knife about six inches long hanging from a sheath on his belt.

"What are you going to do if we meet a bear, try to stab it with the knife?" Miranda asked.

"Nope." Slim walked over to a stand of bushes, pulled out the knife, and hacked away at a branch about five feet long until it came free. He held it out in front of him. "Sometimes this will drive off a black bear. Unless they have cubs or a fresh kill, they don't usually attack people. They're usually quite timid. Doesn't work so well with a grizzly."

"Then you'll have to get a bigger stick," Miranda teased.

Slim resheathed the knife, strode back to his horse, and swung into the saddle. He dug his heels into the horse's sides, and it began moving off at a good pace on a path around the lake. Walter and Miranda had no choice but to mount their horses and ride after him.

The trail led around the lake and across the rest of the cleared area, and then plunged once more into the woods. The trees were evergreens, and a carpet of needles muffled the sound of the horses' hooves. In places, the trail was narrowed by encroaching bushes, and they had to ride single file. As the afternoon wore on and the sun slipped lower in the sky, they rode mostly in shadow, dappled occasionally by spots of light. The horses moved at a sure-footed, steady pace requiring little guidance from the riders. The trail kept to the right side of the valley, for the most part avoiding the meadows and swampy areas in the center of the valley they occasionally glimpsed through the trees. The ground seemed mostly level, with only a gentle rise.

Around four in the afternoon, they came to a fork branching off to the left, and Slim turned down it, Walter and Miranda following. The trail wound through more trees and then came out into a shrubby meadow dominated by a good-sized lake, swampy around the edges.

"Look!" Miranda enthused. "There's a beaver lodge."

The lodge was a large one, located about twenty feet from shore on the far side of the lake.

Slim pointed to the lower end of the lake. "Dam's over there. There's beaver at places all up the valley till here. Beaver aren't usually found this high up in the mountains. They can only be here 'cause the lake doesn't freeze all the way to the bottom in winter. Either 'cause there's a hot spring somewhere feeding into the lake or 'cause this lake's deeper than most."

"Hot spring!" Miranda enthused, stretching. "Can we find it?"

"If you're thinking of swimming there," Slim said, "I wouldn't. You don't want to get beaver fever. We never found the hot springs around the edge of the lake, so it must feed in under the surface if it's there at all."

"Oh," Miranda said, disappointment evident in her voice. "No hot spring."

"Could just be the lake's deep."

"Isn't this a beaver pond? Didn't the beaver make it?" Miranda asked.

"Possible," Slim answered. "Or maybe there was already a lake, and their dam just made it deeper."

"You sound like a tour guide." Miranda's laughed.

Slim shrugged. "You paid for a trail ride. I'm supposed to tell you stuff like that."

Miranda put on a serious face. "We only paid for four hours. Are you going to charge us extra?"

Slim shrugged again. "I don't get the money anyway. I'm not charging you nothing."

They rode on for a bit in silence.

"Over there," Slim said, pointing to a level area on the right side of the lake. "We'll camp there tonight."

"Why are we stopping so soon?" Walter injected. "We can keep riding."

"It gets dark early in the mountains, and there are things we have to do. There's no streetlights up here, so we have to get them done while we can still see."

Without another word, Slim rode toward the flat, grassy area. There he loosened the two straps holding the lassos on his horse and dismounted.

"Walter," Slim said, "bring your ropes."

When Walter got to where Slim was, Slim had tied the end of one of his ropes about waist high to a tree about six inches thick.

"Tie your rope to the same tree about the height of your head," Slim said.

Slim walked about ten feet, pulled his rope tight, wrapped it around another tree, and moved forward another ten feet, repeating the process. Walter, catching on to the idea, followed along behind, tying his rope to the same trees but considerably higher. When Slim had completed a large semi-circle, he reached the end of the rope and tied it off. Then he took his second rope and did the same thing, completing the circle and ending at the original tree. When both men had finished, the three horses were enclosed in a makeshift corral made of two strands of rope. The ground inside the enclosure was covered with grass and small shrubs. A brook about two feet wide cut across one edge of the corral.

"Take the saddles and bridles off your horses and put them over there," Slim said, indicating a spot just outside the enclosure. "Then follow this water up to where it comes out of the side of the hill and fill up the canteens."

Walter and Miranda stared at Slim for a moment, then obeyed the order. When they got back, they saw that Slim had unfurled the extra roll of material that had been on the back of his horse. It turned out to be a tarp about ten feet by fourteen. He had tied two corners to trees ten feet apart and about four feet up. The other end of the tarp was stretched out on the ground.

"Give me a hand with these," Slim said to Walter. He indicated a couple of fallen logs about four inches thick. They hoisted them up, placing them in the crook of trees about four feet off the ground along the sides of the tarp. Then they placed the saddles and saddle blankets on the two logs.

"Keeps the saddles out of the wet grass and cuts the wind on us," Slim said.

Then Slim walked over to some other trees and began hacking off the finer branches with his knife. "Put those under the tarp," he said, "and then pull the back end of the tarp over top of the branches and put your sleeping bags on top of the bottom layer of the tarp. It won't be the best bed you've ever slept on, but probably won't be the worst neither. Put your coats on top of the sleeping bags for extra warmth."

Finally, Slim used his knife to clear the grass and shrubs away from a space in front of the open end of the tarp. "Go find some rocks about as big as you can carry and put them around here," he said.

When the rocks were in place, Slim started a fire. Then he pulled some pans out of the large canvas bags that had been on his horse and began cooking beans and oatmeal and coffee, with the pans and coffee pot balanced on rocks above the fire.

All three were hungry after their long day, and the simple meal tasted surprisingly good. They ate in silence, drinking in the view of the valley, the trees, the lake, and the mountains. Slim was sitting on a short log. Walter and Miranda had finally taken off their backpacks and were sitting on them. A couple of times, they caught a glimpse of beaver swimming in the water.

By the time they had finished eating, the sun had gone down. Slim used another rope to hang their remaining food supplies in a tree about a hundred feet away.

"To keep it safe from bears," Slim said. "Time to turn in."

Slim crawled into his sleeping bag under one side of the tarp. Walter took the other outside position, with Miranda in the middle.

"Are we going to take turns keeping watch?" Miranda asked.

"You can if you want," Slim answered. "I'm going to sleep."

"But isn't it dangerous?" Miranda insisted.

"Isn't what dangerous?" Slim answered. "I don't think the bank robbers will follow us all the way up here. And, as I said, bears don't attack people. They're usually more scared of us than we are of them. About the only thing that could happen is that the beaver might come over and chew off our legs."

"Do beaver do that?" she asked.

"Sure, sometimes. Happened to a friend of mine." Slim paused. "Of course, he was a special case. He had a wooden leg."

There was a long silence. Finally, Miranda said, "Ah, I bet you tell that story to all the tourists."

"Lofty does," Slim murmured.

*****

They awoke cold and stiff. No animals had disturbed their sleep, and they still had all of their limbs. Slim rekindled the fire and began making beans and oatmeal and coffee again. As he was cooking, Walter and Miranda rolled up the tarp and the sleeping bags. The meal tasted even better in the crisp morning air than it had the night before. When it was done, Walter and Miranda put on their backpacks and went off to refill the canteens at the spring while Slim cleaned up the dishes. Then they resaddled the horses and gathered up the ropes that had made the corral.

As they rode past the lake and back onto the main trail, they passed some freshly cut trees. They paused and looked back toward the pond. They could see a couple of vees on the surface of the water that indicated beaver swimming.

"I'm just glad it wasn't one of the trees we used for the corral," Slim said and then urged his horse forward.

The previous day, the trail had seemed generally flat with a slight upward tendency. On this second day, that changed. The gentle slope had become less gentle, and they were climbing higher with every step the horses took. After an hour or so, the trees began to thin. After another hour, the trees became shorter and more scattered. Eventually, they emerged into an area where there were bushes but no trees.

"This is called an alpine meadow or sometimes alpine tundra. We are apparently above the tree line. It is not thought that this area is too cold for trees to grow, but the cold, the wind, the heavy snowpack, and occasional avalanches make it hard for trees to survive."

To Miranda, it seemed to be one of the longest and most technical speeches she had heard Slim make. But it was delivered like a recitation. It was part of the tour.

Miranda shivered. The strength of the wind had increased, and the temperature was definitely a few degrees cooler than the day before.

They rode on, along the edge of the meadow. After another half hour, Slim pulled up and began staring across to the other side of the valley. He retrieved a pair of binoculars from his saddlebag and began scanning the steep slope.

Handing the binoculars to Miranda, he said, "Look a little to the left and about two-thirds of the way up."

Miranda took the binoculars and began scanning the slope for herself. After about half a minute, she exclaimed, "I see them! What are they?"

"Dall sheep," Slim answered. "They prefer the higher altitudes, and on the steep slopes they are safer from wolves and bears and mountain lions."

"They move so quickly!" Miranda exclaimed.

"Yeah, they're even more sure-footed than Molly," Slim answered.

"But why are they called dolls?" Miranda asked.

"I think they're named after some scientist who first saw them or something," Slim answered.

Miranda passed the binoculars to Walter, but he handed them back after a perfunctory look.

They rode forward the rest of the morning through alpine meadows, always angling upward. Finally, Slim dismounted beside a small stream babbling down the side of the valley.

"Time to let the horses drink and graze for a bit," he said. "Have some jerky if you're hungry."

Miranda and Walter dismounted too. They all walked around for a few minutes, stretching aching muscles. They ate and drank a little and refilled the canteens from the stream. It was almost routine by now. They did what was expected without Slim having to tell them what to do.

After a final stretch, Slim sauntered over to his horse and took hold of the reins again, then swung easily up into the saddle. Walter and Miranda did the same, a little less easily.

"See how the valley curves off to the left," Slim said. "We're going to cut across the meadow to the slope over there. See the trail going up the right side. That leads up to the pass."

Walter immediately urged his horse forward, heading directly for the place where the trail began. As she often did, Miranda rode beside Slim.

"What's your story, Slim?" Miranda asked after a while.

"My story?" Slim answered.

"Yes, your story. Your life. What have you done? How did you get here?"

Slim was silent for a moment. "Not much of a story. Grew up a couple of hundred miles from here. Small town. Just me and my Mom. Didn't like school. After high school, I got this job." There was a further silence. Then Slim asked, "How about you? What's your story?"

Miranda laughed that alluring laugh. "I don't have much of a story either. I grew up in the city. We were just an average family. I have an older brother and a younger sister. After high school, I worked for a couple of years. Then I met Walter, fell in love, and got married. And now we're on our honeymoon!"

"What about Walter? What's his?"

Miranda didn't laugh this time. "Oh, Walter's different. He's smart. He can do anything he wants to do."

"He's older than you."

"Just a few years. Walter's been places, done things."

"It's odd," Slim said.

"What's odd?"

Slim shrugged. "You seem badly matched. Like a draught horse and a pony hitched together."

Miranda suddenly kicked her horse forward and galloped ahead to ride beside Walter.

When they had crossed the meadow, the others stopped, waiting for Slim to catch up.

Slim took the trail coat that was draped in front of his saddle. "It gets colder up on the ridge," he said. "You'll need your coats."

Walter and Miranda pulled on their coats over their backpacks. Slim took the lead. It was single file now, along a trail angling steeply up the side of the valley. When he reached the top, Slim turned his horse to the right, and a long, narrow, flat area stretched before them. The wind whistled across the ridge, tugging at their coats and hats. It was difficult to talk.

Slim continued to lead. After a half hour, the land slowly began to slope downward, like a large bowl. They were descending into the head of another valley. There were still no trees, just grass and bushes. A small stream had begun somewhere and was trickling down the valley beside them.

When the trail widened, Miranda fell in beside Slim again.

"Do you have a girlfriend, Slim?" she asked.

Slim turned to look at her. "No."

"Why not? Young, good-looking guy like you?"

"Look around. The only females I see on a regular basis are horses."

"And occasional tourists on trail rides."

"And occasional tourists on trail rides," Slim agreed. He looked straight ahead.

The land sloped continually downward, and a few short trees began to appear. The air began to feel a little warmer even though the sun was dropping lower in the sky, and they took off their trail coats.

"Over there," Slim said.

He led them to the side of the valley where a small tributary flowed toward the main stream through a stand of scattered trees. He dismounted, tied his horse's reins to a tree branch, and began laying out the rope corral once again. Walter took his rope and began attaching the second strand of the corral.

As they were finishing, a strong crosswind began blowing across the valley, making the grass, trees, and bushes sway violently. Suddenly the horses began neighing and pulling at their reins. They were staring wild-eyed across to a small gully on the other side of the valley.

"Better check it out," Slim said.

He began walking across the valley toward the gully. Walter and Miranda walked a little behind him and a few feet to the side, one on each side of him. As they walked, they kept looking around and ahead, trying to see anything that might have spooked the horses.

"Maybe it was just the wind," Slim said.

Miranda was on the left, where the ground sloped upward, putting her a few feet higher than the others.

"It's a sheep," she said.

"A dead sheep," Walter said.

"A kill," Slim said. "Back away slowly right now!"

A dark shadow rose up out of the hollow behind the dead sheep.

"Grizzly bear!" Slim said urgently. "Back away now!"

All three of them were moving swiftly backwards, while trying to look as large and as formidable as possible. The bear lowered its head and began moving forward. As Slim passed a small stand of scrub, he began hacking furiously at one of the small trees with his knife. About an inch and a half thick and ten feet long, it finally broke free with a loud crack. The bear was charging forward at full speed by this time, roaring in fury as it approached the three intruders. Frantically, Slim waved his makeshift weapon directly in the path of the oncoming bear, still backing away as swiftly as he could. The bear continued its charge undeterred. Suddenly, there was a loud explosion, followed by several more. The charging bear lowered its head, did a somersault, and lay still. The bear lay on its back underneath Slim's branch, its back claws about four feet from Slim.

Slim looked around. Miranda was holding a large handgun in her outstretched hand, shaking a little. Walter, on Slim's other side, was holding a similar handgun, as steady as a rock. Their backpacks were at their feet. Slim stared at them, his mouth open.

"We're from the city," Miranda said.

"There are a lot of wild animals in the city too," Walter said.

"We're on our honeymoon," Miranda said.

"We came prepared for an adventure," Walter added.

Slim stepped over and stared down at the dead bear. "One of you is a great shot," he said. "Or very lucky. Several bullets hit him in the head, and one hit him in the eye. It probably went right through into the brain. That's probably the one that killed him."

"Are you going to cut him up? Are we going to eat bear steak tonight?" Miranda asked.

"I don't know anything about butchering a bear," Slim answered. "And I don't want to be anywhere near here when it gets dark. We've got to get out of here."

"How hard can it be?" Miranda demanded.

"That's not the point," Slim answered. "By nightfall, these two carcasses are going to attract every bear and mountain lion and wolf in the area. Unless you two want to spend the night fighting off wild animals, we've got to get out of here."

"But couldn't we just take some of the meat?" Miranda asked.

"The other animals will smell the blood and follow our trail right down to our camp," Slim insisted. "Do you want that?"

"Are you just going to leave the bear here?" Miranda asked incredulously.

"Yep," Slim answered.

"But couldn't we just pack all that meat out?" Miranda asked.

"I don't have a hunting license," Slim said. "Do you?"

"But we shot the bear in self-defense!" Miranda said. "We shouldn't get into trouble for that."

"No," Slim answered. "We wouldn't. But we would have to spend a lot of time explaining that to the conservation officers, maybe even bringing them back here to show them how it happened. And once there is an investigation, there would be stories about it in the newspapers and on TV. Do you really want all that hassle?"

"He's right," Walter said. "We've got to go, Miranda."

Reluctantly, she turned away. "But can I at least tell my friends that I shot a grizzly bear?"

"Sure," Slim answered. "As long as they are a long way from here and you leave me out of it."

"It certainly has been an adventure," Miranda said smugly.

They returned to the horses and unstrung their makeshift corral. Slim and Walter worked quickly while Miranda watched, holding the horses' reins. The horses were still moving around uneasily and pulling on the reins. No one said anything.

When the ropes were coiled, they remounted. Slim led them down the right side of the valley, well away from the carcasses. They rode quickly, trying to cover as much ground as possible before dark. Finally, Slim turned off to the right, where another stream was trickling down the mountain slope. They had travelled several miles, and they re-erected their tarp shelter by the light of the fire Slim lit.

Nothing was said over dinner. The beans and oatmeal didn't taste as good as they had the night before. They remained sitting there after the meal was over.

"What are you going to do after we reach the Lazy C?" Walter asked at last. "I suppose you'll contact the police as soon as you can get to a phone and tell them what happened to Lofty and the Majors."

"Well, now," Slim said. He took off his hat and scratched his head. "I don't know if I will."

There was a pause. Then Slim spoke again. "I never heard a shot."

"What? When we shot the bear?" Walter asked.

"No. When we were up on the ridge looking back at the ranch," Slim said. "I never heard a shot."

"So?" Walter asked. "I thought I did. We were quite far away."

"No," Slim said. "I didn't hear a shot because I don't think there was a shot. I don't think Lofty was shot. I think he was lying on the ground because he was told to lie on the ground.

I don't think I need to call the cops because I think they were already there."

"What?!" Miranda demanded. "You think the men in the black SUV were police instead of bank robbers?"

"Yep," Slim said.

"Then why didn't we just go back down to the ranch?" Miranda Insisted. "Why did you make us go on this dangerous three-day ride with beavers and grizzly bears?"

"You wanted an adventure," Slim countered. "And you didn't have to pay for it. You got what you wanted."

"But you lied to us!" Miranda said. "You should have given us the choice."

"I didn't want to do that," Slim said.

"What makes you think those guys were the police?" Walter asked.

"Because Lofty and the Majors weren't just raising hay and giving trail rides," Slim said. "I was paid to help out with that. But in the other buildings I found out they were growing marijuana. They'd been doing it for years. They used to smuggle marijuana bundles out in the middle of loads of hay. I figured the cops were there to bust the grow-up."

"Why would you think that?" Miranda asked.

"Because I made a phone call from the Coopers' place a couple of weeks ago when we had the last trail ride," Slim said. "I didn't want to get caught up in that."

"So, you made us take a long trail ride just so you wouldn't get caught in a raid you set up?" Miranda demanded.

"Yep," Slim said. "That's about it."

"But you worked there," Walter said. "The police will find that out and come looking for you."

"No, they won't," Slim answered. "My wages were paid in cash, under the table, out of the drug money is my guess. There is no record I was ever at that ranch."

"But you'll have to go back to get your clothes and things," Miranda protested.

"No, I won't," Slim answered. "I brought my money and everything important with me. All I left behind was some old work clothes. I can replace those easy enough. I've had my saddlebags packed and ready to go for a week. When you drove in, I thought you might be the cops, so I grabbed my saddlebags and had my horse saddled before Lofty called me to take you on the trail ride."

"What if we had been the police?" Miranda asked.

"I would have done exactly what I did," Slim answered, "slipped out of the back of the barn and taken the trail over the mountains to the Lazy C."

"What are you going to do when you get there?" Miranda asked.

Slim shrugged. "Leave the horses at the ranch, get a ride out to the highway, catch a bus, and go off to start a new life." Slim paused. "But what about you? Your car is back at the ranch. What are you going to say when the cops come looking for you?"

Miranda and Walter looked at each other.

"It's not our car. It's a rental," Miranda said.

"It's probably back at the rental company by now," Walter added.

"But there's a rental agreement with your name on it. The cops'll come looking for you as soon as they see it."

There was a pause.

"Funny thing about that car," Walter said. "We picked it up at the airport…"

"We were on an adventure," Miranda interposed, "so we hadn't reserved the car ahead of time."

"When we rented the car, the rental company was having trouble with its computers. There was a long lineup, and the clerks were getting flustered, trying to keep everybody happy," Walter said. "We signed the contract and got out of there. The next day we happened to look at the contract and realized the previous renter's name and address were still on it. We figured we would sort it out when we brought the car back."

"But you signed the contract," Slim suggested.

"Walter's signature?" Miranda released that alluring bubbling laugh. "Good luck trying to read that squiggle!"

"What about your belongings in the car?" Slim asked.

"We're on an adventure and traveling light," Miranda answered. "Everything we need is in our backpacks. The only thing we left in the car is a couple of empty coffee cups."

"There's no record of us ever being at that ranch either," Walter said.

"So, what are you going to do tomorrow?" Slim asked. "Are you going to call the cops?"

"Why should we?" Walter said. "We don't know anything about any grow-op."

"We'll just ask for a ride to the highway like you and go on with our adventure!" Miranda enthused.

A wolf howled in the distance, and Miranda shivered.

"Best get to bed," Slim said. "Another hard ride tomorrow."

*****

They awoke the next morning even more stiff and sore than the day before. By now, they knew the routine. They were back in the saddle by the time the sun had fully risen over the ridge of mountains.

The trail continued on along the right edge of the valley, which began to slope downward more steeply. By mid-morning, they were back among trees. A misty rain had begun falling, glistening on their hats and trail coats. They ate lunch in the saddle, more beef jerky and trail mix. Around mid-afternoon they came out of the trees and were looking down on a broad valley full of hayfields.

"That's the Coopers' ranch house down there," Slim said, pointing to a cluster of dark rectangular smudges on the horizon at the far edge of the hayfields.

They kicked their horses on, but it was still close to an hour before they rode into the open space in the middle of the cluster of buildings. Slim led the way through a big set of doors into a massive horse barn.

A gray-haired, bronze-faced man approached them. He was pleasantly round and walked with that rolling gait common among men who had spent a lot of time in the saddle. His round face broke into a smile, showing uneven, off-white teeth.

"Afternoon, Slim," he said. "Had a good ride?"

"Yep," Slim said. "Last ride of the season. Phil Cooper, this is Walter and Miranda." After a pause, he added. "They're on their honeymoon and wanted an adventure."

"Welcome to the Lazy C," Phil said. "Why don't you two go on over to the kitchen in the big house. Maggie'll get you some coffee. Slim and I'll take care of the horses."

"Thank you so much!" Miranda babbled.

Walter and Miranda walked stiffly back through the rain and in through the front door of the house.

Maggie turned out to be as round and as gray and as cheerful as her husband. "Come on in," she called from the door of the kitchen. "Sit yourselves down, and I'll get you some coffee."

They were finishing the coffee just as Slim and Phil came in from the barn.

"I bet you'd like to get cleaned up," Maggie said to Miranda and Walter. "Room to the left at the top of the stairs. There's fresh towels in the bathroom and a shower big enough for two." She winked.

Miranda laughed that infectious laugh, grabbed Walter's hand, and ran with him up the stairs.

When they came back down, Maggie had set the big dining table in the main room, and exciting smells were coming from the kitchen.

"I hope you like venison stew and fresh cornbread," Maggie said from the doorway.

"Oh, yes!" Miranda laughed. "Anything would be better than Slim's oatmeal and beans!"

Over dinner, they talked about the trail ride over the pass, the beavers, and the adventure with the grizzly bear. Phil and Maggie talked about their ranch. Phil had inherited it from his father, and for the past thirty-five years they had operated it together, raising beef cattle, growing hay, and accommodating tourists looking for an authentic ranch experience. They had raised four children there, all now off to schools and jobs elsewhere.

"And what are your plans?" Maggie asked Walter and Miranda.

"Well, right now, we'd like to get on with our adventure. Do you think we could get a ride down to the highway?"

"Why don't you get a good night's sleep upstairs, and we can give you a ride down in the morning," Phil suggested. "There's a Greyhound goes by mid-morning."

"As long as the ride isn't on a horse, that would be great!" Miranda laughed, rubbing her aching thighs.

*****

Breakfast was pancakes, eggs, bacon, and coffee.

"No oatmeal or beans?" Miranda laughed.

When they came back down after breakfast, Slim was waiting for them in the big room.

"Phil's offered me a job," Slim said. "I'm going to be staying here at the Lazy C. My first duty is to drive you down to the highway."

They walked out through the big front door into warm sunshine, the misty rain having blown away.

A big new gray pickup was standing in front of the house.

"Shotgun!" Miranda called and climbed up into the front seat of the truck beside Slim.

Walter stumbled into the back seat of the club cab. The big truck cruised smoothly out onto the road and began winding down the paved side road toward the highway. The seats were soft, the temperature warm, and the country music on the radio soft and mournful.

"This truck is more sure-footed than Molly," Miranda laughed after a while.

"And shinier," Slim agreed.

They rode on for another few miles, the warm fall sun filling the cab of the truck.

"How did you convince Phil to hire you?" Miranda asked after a while.

"No problem," Slim said. "He knows me from other trail rides through to his place—and I told him he could keep the three horses."

"But they're not your horses," Miranda protested.

"The Major's not going to need them back," Slim said. "He's going to jail."

"He is?" Miranda asked. "So, it *was* the police who came to the farm?"

"Oh, yeah. Phil said it's been all over the news," Slim said. "Turns out Major's not his real name, and he was wanted for some other stuff he did years ago someplace else."

"Could the Major and Lofty be the bank robbers too?" Miranda asked.

"News didn't say nothing about that," Slim answered.

"What do you think, Walter?" Miranda asked.

There was no answer. Miranda turned to look into the back. Walter was slumped over.

"Walter?" Miranda turned back to look at Slim. "What did you do to Walter?!"

"He's alright. Just a couple of sleeping pills in his coffee."

"Why?!"

"Just to be sure. Didn't want to take any chances."

The truck cruised around another curve and up over a small hill. The side road wound out before them heading for the highway a few miles away. Several cars appeared to be parked at the junction of the two roads.

Miranda sat up sharply. "Are those police cars?" she asked.

"Looks like," Slim answered. "Probably a roadblock looking for those bank robbers."

Miranda grabbed her backpack from the floor of the pickup and began unzipping the central compartment.

"Won't do you no good pulling out that gun," Slim said calmly. "Phil and I took out the bullets while you were taking your shower yesterday."

"What do you mean?" Miranda asked.

"We also saw the money that was in there," Slim said.

"Did you take that too?" Miranda asked, looking frantically into the backpack."

"Nah, it's still there," Slim said.

"How did you know?" Miranda asked.

"What? That you two were the bank robbers?" Slim asked. "Wasn't hard. Two people, dressed in black, medium height, carrying handguns."

"If we hadn't shot the grizzly, you never would have guessed, would you?" Miranda asked.

"Maybe," Slim said. "But if you hadn't shot the grizzly, it probably would have eaten you."

"Stupid bear!" Miranda muttered.

"Don't blame the bear," Walter protested. "The bear was just doing what bears do. Besides, I was already suspicious. Remember I spent the last year and a half with a bunch of crooks pretending to be somebody else. I could see the signs. Why would you be on a deserted road going nowhere? Why were you holding on to those backpacks so hard? Why'd you make up that story about hearing a shot and saying right off that the guys in the SUV must be the bank robbers? It was obvious you were hiding something."

"You don't have to say anything to the police, Slim," Miranda said. "They don't have the same reasons to be suspicious. They'll probably let us go right through the roadblock if you don't say anything."

"Not going to happen," Slim said. "They're waiting for you. I called them last night. Bank offered a reward, you know."

"But it's probably not nearly as much as what we have in these backpacks," Miranda said. "We could give you half. You could just say you made a mistake, or you could turn around before they see us."

"If I wanted the money, I could just have taken it and left you out in the mountains."

"But we had the guns," Miranda argued.

"Didn't matter," Slim said. "I could have taken off with the horses sometime when you were getting water. No food and no shelter in the middle of the mountains, a hundred and fifty miles from anywhere, you'd never have made it out. I could have gone back later and picked up the money." He paused. "Or I could have slit your throats with the knife in the middle of one of those nights when we weren't keeping watch."

"How are you going to tell the police about the trail ride?" Miranda asked. "That will tie you to the grow-op at the other ranch."

"What trail ride?" Slim asked. "I've been working at the Lazy C for the last two months. You and Walter showed up there last night, and we have no idea where you came from or how you got there. According to what I'll tell the cops, your adventure never happened, Miranda."

Miranda's eyes flashed with anger. Then they softened. She gently placed her hand on Slim's thigh.

"You wouldn't want to see me go to prison, would you? Prisons are horrible places," she whispered. "The robbery was all Walter's idea. I was very foolish, but I was young and in love. I don't know why I went along with it. When we get to the police, turn Walter in with one of the backpacks. I'll back you up. We'll tell them that we don't know where the other robber is or that he died in the mountains and a grizzly bear ate him. Then you and I can take the other backpack and go away together. You'd like that, wouldn't you, Slim?"

Slim smiled and leaned closer to Miranda. He said softly, "You'd betray your husband on your honeymoon? If he is your husband. If it is your honeymoon."

Slim continued, "If you'd betray Walter, you'd betray me, first chance you got. I'm starting to think the robbery was your idea, and you convinced Walter to do it. Sorry, Miranda, but I don't trust you. The honeymoon is over."

The shiny, gray pickup pulled in beside the police cars and stopped.

Anniversary Cruise

"I want to ask you a question," John Smyth said. "Actually, several questions."

"Yes, you have to go to work. No, we can't sell the children. Yes, we have to go to the school play tonight instead of watching the hockey game. And no, I'm not going to tell you what we're having for dinner," his wife Ruby answered.

"Thank you for that," John said, "but I have a couple of different questions, serious ones."

"Okay, but I don't guarantee you will like the answers."

"We've been married almost twenty-five years," John began.

"Good for you. You've been keeping track."

"Are you disappointed that I still have the same job?"

"Being editor of *Grace* magazine is an important job, and many people in Grace Evangelical churches benefit from your work. Besides, I'm glad that you still have a job of any kind."

"Are you saying that I'm not very employable?" John demanded.

Ruby smiled.

"Seriously, are you disappointed that we are still living in this same small house in inner-city Winnipeg?" John asked earnestly.

Ruby was silent for a moment. "When we got married, I agreed it was for better or worse. Our house could be better, but it could also be a lot worse. At least, we have a house."

"Are you angry that I've gotten involved in solving a number of murders over the years?"

"I wasn't happy about it, but at least you weren't the one committing the murders."

"Do you still love me?"

"Yes."

"Why?"

"Well, John, you are going to have to realize that there are some mysteries that even you cannot solve."

"I have another question for you," John said. "How would you like to go on a cruise with me?"

"John, we can't afford that."

"I know, but the board has offered to pay most of the cost for us to take a cruise out of gratitude for my twenty years of service."

"Can they use church money for that?"

"They aren't using church money. They and a few other people kicked in some money out of their own pockets."

"I thought you said the board doesn't like you."

"I guess I was wrong. I guess they love me too," John said. "And I think some of them might have agreed to it knowing that the ship might hit a rock and sink."

"Where would we go on this cruise?"

"The board is suggesting the Inside Passage."

"What? Inside what?"

"It's a cruise that starts in Vancouver and goes north between the coast of British Columbia and the islands offshore. They call it the Inside Passage because it's inside the islands. The sea is calmer there, and there are spectacular views of the coastal mountains."

"Sounds wonderful."

"The cruise continues on from there, north to Alaska."

"I've seen the movie, and you are John Smyth, not John Wayne. He was taller and handsomer and had more money."

"The story's not about money. It's about love. Remember the song in that movie: *'I'd trade all the gold that's buried in this land for one small band of gold to put on sweet little Jenny's hand.'*"

"I've heard the song, and you're not Johnny Horton either. In fact, you're not much of a singer of any kind."

"I might not have found gold in Alaska, but I found a Ruby."

"You're not a comedian either."

"No, but I am a very blessed man."

"That you are."

Day One

John and Ruby walked down a remarkably long corridor, passing through doorways in multiple bulkheads, which made it look as if they were between two mirrors with the reflections diminishing into infinity. At the end of the corridor, they reached a wide hallway extending across the width of the ship. This in turn gave access to a broad, curved stairway leading down to the level of the dining room. At the bottom of the stairs, they entered a vast room filled with round tables set with starched, white tablecloths and sparkling silverware.

"We need to find Table 29," John said. "I think that means we will be sitting at the same table with the same people every night at dinner. I wonder why they set it up that way."

"Maybe the idea is that we will get to sit with people we know instead of sitting with a new group of strangers every night," Ruby suggested.

"That only works if we get along with the people at our table. If we don't, it could be a long three weeks."

"It's only a one-week cruise."

"I know, but it will seem longer."

"We're just going to have to take the initiative and start the conversation," Ruby said.

"That doesn't sound like us."

"Maybe we'll have to step out of character for once. There it is." Ruby indicated a table ahead of them.

Ten of the twelve chairs were vacant. The other two were occupied by a middle-aged couple. The man was of medium height, had a reddish-blond mustache, and was dressed in an inexpensive gray suit. The woman was slightly shorter, with dark, shoulder-length hair, and was wearing a plain, navy blue dress. John and Ruby sat in the chairs to their right. The man half rose awkwardly to greet them. John extended his right hand toward the man.

"Hello. I'm John Smyth, and this is my wife, Ruby."

"Bob Coates," the man said, taking the extended hand. "And Janet."

"I'm pleased to meet you," Ruby said, smiling at Janet. "We just flew in from Winnipeg. This is our first cruise."

"We're from Douglas River in the interior of British Columbia," Bob said. "It's our first cruise too."

Another couple were approaching the table. They were slim and of medium height and appeared to be in their late twenties. They moved with a formal grace. They were obviously together but were not touching or talking. They sat down opposite Bob and Janet, leaving two empty chairs between them and Ruby and four empty chairs on the other side.

"Hi." Ruby smiled. "We're Ruby and John."

"We're Bob and Janet, well, actually Janet and Bob," Janet said, gesturing.

The new couple both started to speak at once, then stopped and looked at each other. Finally, the man said, "I'm Aiden King, and this is my wife, Alicia."

"Alicia, that's a very pretty name." Ruby smiled again.

The conversation stalled as a fourth couple approached the table. The man was close to six feet tall, had powerful shoulders, and was dressed in a powder blue silk suit. A thick gold chain was visible at his open-necked shirt. There were several gold rings on his fingers, but not on the finger that communicated anything. The woman was shorter, with a full figure. She was wearing a red leather dress with a bodice cut low and a skirt cut high. ("The dressmaker saved cloth at both ends," Ruby later observed to John.) The new couple sat down in the two empty chairs between the Smyths and the Kings.

When those already at the table had introduced themselves, the man spoke in a strong voice. "I'm Dion, and she's Celeste."

Celeste smiled.

"Where are you from?" John asked.

"I'm from Vancouver," Dion said.

Another couple were approaching the table. He was dressed in a dark suit and a white shirt, and she was dressed in a tight silk dress.

"Lordy, Lordy, Letitia," the man boomed as they reached the table. "Dey done put us at de white folks' table!"

"Don't be a fool, Elroy," the woman responded. "Dem dwarves over dhere might be lily white, but most of de rest o' dem looks like dey's got some color in dheir backgrounds somewheres."

The two of them looked at each other and burst into laughter. Those around the table sat in shocked silence.

"Please excuse my husband," Letitia said in a more cultured southern accent. "My husband has a perverted sense of humor."

"I find a little humor is useful in building rapport with my students," Elroy said, "and it can help break the ice in other social situations as well."

"I concur," John Smyth said. "I find that most people in new social situations adopt a persona that is quite distinct from their true selves. My wife Ruby and I, for instance, often pretend to be short when we are both actually well over six feet tall."

Elroy looked at John and laughed. "I perceive you also have a sense of humor."

"More humor than sense most days," Ruby said.

This time, everyone at the table joined in the laughter.

"Allow me to give a proper introduction. I'm Elroy Simmons. I'm a high school principal in Atlanta, Georgia, and my wife, Letitia, is a school counselor."

"We're taking this cruise to celebrate our twentieth wedding anniversary," Letitia added.

"We're John and Ruby Smyth from Winnipeg, Manitoba," John said. "And we are ahead of you in the marriage department. We're taking this cruise to celebrate our twenty-fifth anniversary."

"It's not a competition," Elroy said.

"Bob and Janet Coates from Douglas River, B.C. We've been married thirteen years," Bob said.

"But we're not celebrating," Janet added.

There was a slight pause, and then laughter rippled around the table again, following Elroy's lead.

"I mean our anniversary is in December, and we're not taking the cruise to celebrate our anniversary," Janet stammered.

"Why are you—?" John started to ask but stopped when Aiden spoke.

"I'm Aiden King, and this is Alicia. We're from Richmond, B.C. That's just south of Vancouver," Aiden said. "We're not celebrating either."

"I'm Dion, and this is Celeste," Dion said. "We're not married, but we're celebrating."

"Celebrating what?" Janet asked.

"We're celebrating being on a cruise."

A final couple approached the table, a tall man with neat, dark hair slightly graying at the temples and a slightly shorter woman with neatly coiffed blonde hair. Their clothes were not flashy but understated and fashionable. His suit was tailored to his well-toned body, and her designer dress fit her perfectly. They sat in the only vacant chairs between Elroy and Letitia and Aiden and Alicia, but before anyone could speak, another man approached the table. He was short and lithe with short, black hair and was dressed in black pants, a white shirt, and a white jacket. He had been hovering nearby for some minutes.

"Good evening," the newcomer said. "I am Roberto, and I am honored to be your waiter this evening. To start, you have your choice of four appetizers: sagaraki flambé, coquilles St. Jacques, smoked salmon canapes, and spiedini."

"I will have the salmon," Elroy said.

When the others had given their orders, Elroy said, "On such occasions, there is usually one English word in there that I can recognize, and I order that."

The next two hours were devoted to the serious business of fine dining. There were seven courses, with at least three options for each one. Between courses, there was just enough time to re-introduce everyone at the table for the benefit of the last arriving couple. It sounded like the roll call of football players near the beginning of NFL games.

"Elroy and Letitia Simmons from Atlanta, Georgia."

"Bob and Janet Coates from Douglas River, B.C."

"Ruby and John Smyth from Winnipeg, Manitoba."

"Dion and Celeste from British Columbia."

"Aiden and Alicia King from Richmond, B.C."

"Thatcher and Autumn Kinkaid from Phoenix, Arizona."

"There will be a test," Elroy said, turning to Thatcher and Autumn. "Repeat everyone's names."

Everyone laughed.

"Some of us are celebrating anniversaries," Elroy said. "What brings you to this cruise?"

"Thatch is a business executive," Autumn said. "He's been in British Columbia for the past few months on a temporary contract, and we thought we would finish off our time there with a cruise."

*****

"Are you glad we came?" John asked later that evening. "Did you enjoy this evening?"

"Oh, yes," Ruby answered." The food was wonderful, and the conversation was fun."

"Yes, it was fun," John agreed. "But was it informative? Didn't it make you curious about the back stories of the people at our table, what they're really like when they're at home, what their families are like, what their problems and issues are?"

"Maybe we'll find out more as the cruise goes on," Ruby said. "But I will tell you one thing. We are going to have to drop to two meals a day, maybe brunch and dinner. If we keep eating like this, they are going to have to roll us off the ship in a wheelbarrow."

Day Two

When they had boarded the ship, they had passed from the terminal over a covered gangway into the bowels of the ship. The stop in Ketchikan, Alaska, late in the afternoon was their first opportunity to see the profile of the ship they were sailing on. As John and Ruby stood on the quay gazing up at

141

the massive ship *Arctic Adventure* looming fourteen stories above them, they were impressed. It was by far the largest manmade structure in the small fishing village. The population on the ship was almost half as large as the population of the whole village.

John and Ruby walked around the village for the next hour, not roaming far from the quay.

"This is silly," Ruby said. "I'm almost afraid to get far from the ship in case it sails without us. Even though we know it's not scheduled to leave for a couple of hours yet."

"I know what you mean," John said. "Feelings aren't necessarily related to reality."

They were just coming out of a small shop when John, looking behind to talk with Ruby, almost collided with another couple coming in. It was Aiden and Alicia King.

"I'm sorry," John apologized.

"That's okay," Alicia replied. "I'm glad we bumped into you."

"We didn't actually collide," John said.

"I meant we're glad we met you. Can we talk to you about something?" Alicia said.

"Sure," John said. "There's a coffee shop. Do you want to go there?"

When they had their coffees and were seated around an outside table, Aiden asked without preamble, "We would like to know...how do you do it?"

"How do we do what?" John asked.

"You've been married twenty-five years, right?" Aiden asked.

"Yes," John said.

"How do you keep the romance alive that long? How did you stay married?" Aiden asked.

"Or are you just staying married out of habit?" Alicia added.

John thought for a moment. "Well, the romance is still there, we still love each other, but why are you asking?"

"We met on a cruise," Alicia said. "It was a work cruise, and it was magic right from the start. But eight years later, well, things just feel stale and boring. The magic has gone."

"Gone?" Ruby asked.

"Yes, it's not the same as it was when we first met," Alicia said.

"Well, I don't think you can recreate the novelty, that unexpected joy when you first got to know each other," Ruby said. "You already know each other. It won't be the same, but that doesn't mean it can't be good."

"You work at the same company?" John said. "Do you have coffee breaks?"

"Sure." Aiden shrugged.

"Do you enjoy them?"

"Yeah, most of the time," Aiden said. "They're a good break from work."

"When you get home at the end of the day, do you think about and talk about the coffee breaks or about the work you did?" John asked.

"Mostly the work, I guess," Aiden said.

"What John is saying is that romance is like the coffee break," Ruby said. "It's fun and enjoyable, but it's not the main thing."

"What is the main thing?" Aiden asked.

"It's working together to build something," Ruby said.

"Build what?" Alicia asked.

"A home. A family. A business. A relationship. A community. A life," Ruby said. "You can't expect a marriage to be all coffee breaks. You'd get bored with a coffee break after more than a few minutes."

"That doesn't mean that we don't still have some pretty good coffee breaks," John added.

"Right," Ruby said. "John still buys me presents and does little things for me and even takes me on a cruise once every twenty-five years or so."

Aiden and Alicia laughed.

"But it's the work we do in between, our shared life together, that makes the breaks special," John said. "Not the other way around."

*****

"So how did you all enjoy Ketchican?" Elroy asked.

"Typical little fishing village," Bob said.

"With fifty jewelry stores," Aiden said.

"Why does a fishing village of only a few thousand people need that many jewelry stores?" Bob asked.

"Look around this table for your answer," Elroy answered. "Those stores aren't there for the fishermen. They're there for us rich tourists. That fishing village lands a boatload of suckers every day."

"Did you see that one store that had the big jade carving of a bear?" Letitia asked. "That thing must have been three feet high, carved out of a single piece of jade."

"Yes, beautiful," Alicia said.

"It must have weighed a ton, literally," Bob said.

"We bought it," Ruby said.

"You bought it? That thing cost more than the whole cruise," Janet said.

"Not that one exactly, but one just like it," Ruby said. She reached into her purse and pulled out a jade carving about an inch high.

Everyone laughed.

"The Kinkaids bought a bigger one," Janet said.

"What?" Elroy asked.

"A bigger one," Janet said. "We were passing by the store, and we saw them buying a bigger one."

"Did you really?" Elroy asked, turning to Thatcher and Autumn.

"We bought a bigger one, but not the big one," Autumn admitted. "Ours was only about a foot high."

"With that many jewelry stores," Elroy said, looking at Dion, "maybe you went looking for engagement rings?"

144

"Marriage is outdated," Dion said. "With all your outdated rules and traditional values, you suck all the joy out of life."

"Stop smiling," Elroy said, tapping Letitia on the arm. "We're supposed to be miserable."

Day Three

"That is amazing," Ruby said.

"Awe-inspiring," John agreed.

They were staring at the sheer, white face of the Hubbard Glacier soaring a few hundred feet into the sky and stretching for four or five miles across the end of a deep bay.

"Do you remember that first day in Ketchikan, when we were standing on the dock and staring up at the ship, feeling small compared to how big the ship was?" John asked.

"You mean that now the ship is tiny compared to the size of the glacier?" Ruby said.

"Right. God is much greater than anything human beings can devise."

"We're on vacation. It's not the time for a theological discussion."

"God never takes a vacation," John said.

"But he rested on the seventh day."

"See. A theological discussion."

"Let's get out of this wind," Ruby said.

Although it was a sunny day, the wind blowing over the glacier and onto the ship was frigid. As John and Ruby rounded the corner to stand in the lea of a wall near the bow of the ship, they nearly collided with Aiden and Alicia.

"This is freezing," Alicia mumbled, her teeth chattering.

"The travel agent told us it would be warm in Alaska this time of year, so we didn't pack any warm clothes," Aiden said.

"I never trust experts or people in authority," Elroy said.

The others turned and saw Elroy and Letitia coming around the corner to join them. They were dressed warmly in parkas and toques and had broad smiles on their faces.

"Does that apply to school principals?" John asked.

"Especially to school principals," Letitia said.

"What about you, John? Did your travel agent tell you that it's warm in Alaska in the summertime?" Elroy asked.

"You find this cold?" John asked, patting the shoulder of his light jacket. "We live in Winnipeg on the Canadian prairies, one of the coldest cities on earth."

"How cold?" Elroy asked.

"In the winter, it gets down near minus forty."

"How about the summer?" Elroy asked.

"In summer, it can get up in the high thirties," John said.

"That's all?" Elroy asked. "That's not very warm, barely above freezing."

"John's just having some fun,' Ruby said. "In Canada, we measure temperature on the Celsius scale, not the Fahrenheit scale."

"Doesn't everybody use Celsius?" John asked with a straight face.

"No, John, we're Canadians, not Americans," Ruby said. "We don't expect everyone else to think and behave just like we do."

"Good one," Elroy said. "So, high thirties Celsius—what's that in Fahrenheit?"

"About a hundred," Ruby said.

"What's minus forty?" Elroy asked.

"Minus forty," Ruby said.

"Yes," Elroy said.

"Right."

"What?"

"Now Ruby's pulling your leg," John said. "Minus forty Celsius is minus forty Fahrenheit. The two scales converge at that point."

"And freeze solid," Ruby added.

"So, Winnipeg is very cold in winter and very hot in summer, the worst of both worlds?" Elroy said.

"As opposed to Atlanta, which is hot in winter and unbearably hot in summer," John said.

"Good point," Elroy said and laughed.

*****

146

"Good evening, all. How was your day?" Roberto asked.

There was a generally positive murmur. It was not clear whether the question had been rhetorical.

"You will have noticed that Mr. and Mrs. Kinkaid are not with us. They have been invited to eat at the captain's table this evening. It is a rare privilege granted only to high profile passengers."

There was a further murmur of oohs and aahs.

"Have you met the Kinkaids before?" John asked.

"I have had the privilege of serving Mr. Kinkaid on two other voyages," Roberto said. "Now, the appetizers for this evening are…"

*****

"What shall we talk about this evening?" Elroy asked after a while. "I suggest we talk a little bit about our families. For instance, Letitia and I have three beautiful daughters and—"

Letitia interrupted to finish his sentence. "And one butt-ugly son who, unfortunately, got his looks from his father."

Elroy sat open-mouthed for a second and then nodded his head. "Sad but true. I might as well enrol him in football. He has nothing to lose."

The others at the table laughed.

"Or hockey," John suggested.

"We don't have much of that in Atlanta," Elroy said. "The ice keeps melting."

"John and I have four children, perfectly balanced, two boys and two girls, and all are very good looking like their parents," Ruby said.

"Even Michael," John said sadly.

"Michael?" Elroy asked.

"Our eldest," John said.

"Let me guess," Elroy said. "Thirteen going on thirty-five?"

"Something like that," John said.

"I've got a whole school full of them," Elroy said.

"We have two boys and a girl," Janet said.

"Any other bids?" Elroy asked, looking at Aiden and Alicia.

The two looked at each other.

"We, um, haven't decided yet," Alicia said.

"You haven't decided how many children you have, or you haven't decided whether to have children?" Elroy asked.

"We haven't decided whether we want to have children," Aiden said quietly.

"Never mind what the little people said," Elroy said. "Children are pure joy and are never any trouble at all."

The others laughed.

"And you?" Elroy asked, looking across the table at Dion and Celeste.

"I don't have any children," Dion said, "that I know about anyway."

This was met with an uncomfortable silence, which was finally broken by Elroy.

"I have already told you that I am a school principal and Letitia is a school counselor," Elroy said. "What do the rest of you do when you are not taking cruises?"

Aiden spoke next. "Alicia and I both work at an IT company."

"So, you do things with computers that none of the rest of us would understand?" Elroy asked.

"Pretty much," Aiden agreed, and everyone laughed.

"And what do you do?" Elroy turned to John. "Let me guess. You're a stand-up comedian?"

"More of a sit-down comedian," Letitia suggested. "He's not tall enough to do stand-up."

"Good one, Letitia," Elroy said.

"It's okay. I'm used to tall people making fun of me," John said. "Actually, I'm editor of *Grace* magazine. It's a magazine for the members of Grace Evangelical churches in North America."

"Is that why you just drink water?" Aiden asked.

"One of those narrow-minded people who try to ruin everyone else's fun," Dion said.

The mood at the table had become serious and tense.

"In the first place, we have never tried to ruin anyone else's fun," John said. "And we don't just drink water. We also drink apple juice, chocolate milk, coffee, tea, and Coca-Cola—that last one only on special occasions and high holy days." He smiled, but no one else did. "The Bible and our church don't say people shouldn't drink alcohol, but they are opposed to drunkenness. The reason we don't drink is only indirectly related to our faith. Ruby and I have chosen not to drink because we have seen too many other people destroy their lives with it."

"Great sermon! Pass the collection plate!" Dion said.

"Don't make fun of the man," Elroy said, looking at Dion. "You're the one spoiling the fun. Letitia and I also go to church." He paused. "What do you do, Dion?"

"I own my own business, some retail outlets," Dion said. "And I have a lot of fun." He raised his glass in salute.

"And you two?" Elroy asked, turning to Bob and Janet.

Bob started to speak and then hesitated.

"Go ahead. You can tell them," Janet said.

"We just lost our jobs," Bob said. "My grandfather moved to Douglas River to work at the Northwest Forest Products sawmill there. My Dad worked there too, and I started after high school. I'm—I was—a sawyer. Janet worked part-time in the office. But a multinational bought out the company and started shutting down mills. That was two months ago. We sold our house because we couldn't pay the mortgage, but we didn't get much for it because there's no work in town. We got just enough to go on this cruise, as sort of a final celebration, or maybe as a way to get started on what comes next. We don't know what we're going to do now."

Day Four

Because of shallow water in the harbor, the massive ship had to anchor offshore, and the passengers were tendered ashore in boats. John and Ruby found themselves on the same tender as Aiden and Alicia.

"This is how the gold seekers arrived after 1898. The port was even less accessible then than it is now," John said. "The first gold was not found in Alaska but across the border in Canada's Yukon territory. Skagway was not a gateway to the Alaskan gold fields but to the Yukon gold fields."

"How do you know?" Aiden asked.

"John is a history buff," Ruby explained. "He's almost old enough to be historic himself."

"I took some history courses, and I read a lot," John said.

Upon arrival onshore, they went immediately to the train station, where an old steam engine sat puffing quietly.

"I hope this will be more of an excursion than the jewelry stores in Ketchikan," Ruby said.

They boarded the train together, it gathered speed slowly, and soon it was rocking through a stand of trees. It wound around some curves and then began ascending up the side of a wide, steep valley.

"The train wasn't here at first, of course," John said. "In fact, there was very little here. If you look down into the valley, you can see a few places where the old trail goes along the valley bottom next to the creek. Thousands of gold seekers walked up that trail. They had to bring in more than a ton of supplies each—it was a requirement imposed by the Canadian government because there were no regular supply lines to the Yukon. It's said that three thousand horses died hauling goods up that trail. There was little for them to eat, and they were worked to death. The gold seekers didn't care about anything other than getting rich."

"That's depressing," Alicia said.

"It is indeed," John said. "History is full of many sad tales."

"Speaking of sad tales," Aiden said after a while. "I mean history says that things often turn out badly, that people often change and do disappointing things. Life is unpredictable."

"Yes," John said, "but I get the feeling you're not talking about history."

"A lot of bad things can happen," Alicia said. "Elroy and Letitia said that one of their kids turned out to be ugly."

"I think they were kidding," John said.

"But were you kidding when you talked about Michael?" Alicia asked.

"Well, no," John admitted. "Michael has had his struggles."

"I don't know exactly what they are, but some kids can turn out really badly," Aiden said. "Some have birth defects, and some get cancer, and some are badly hurt in accidents."

"I don't think I could handle that," Alicia said.

"And even marriage is uncertain," Aiden said. "We have friends who were married for less time than we've been, and they are already divorced. Alicia's best friend's boyfriend became a drug addict and ended up dead on the street. Another friend's husband left her for another woman."

"I see," John said, "and you're afraid something like that could happen to you."

"You're afraid to bring children into a world where bad things happen," Ruby added.

"Yes!" Alicia said.

John nodded. "There's a verse in the Bible that says, 'Whoever watches the wind will not plant; whoever looks at the clouds will not reap.' It means that we can become so afraid of what might happen that we don't take a chance. But not taking a chance is the biggest risk of all. The farmer who is so afraid that he doesn't plant seeds is guaranteed to never have a crop. Sure, a crop might fail—it happens—but not taking a chance guarantees failure."

"Marriage is risky," Ruby said. "You are taking the chance that it might turn out badly, but there is also the chance that it might turn out very well."

"I have a friend," John said. "His wife developed Parkinson's disease, and he has spent the last twenty-five years taking care of her."

"That's just it," Aiden said. "I don't think I could do that."

"You know what my friend says?" John said. "He said he feels very blessed that he has been able to have had this wonderful, caring relationship with his wife for twenty-five years."

"You might think it would be very hard to care for an invalid spouse," Ruby said, "but if you were the invalid, wouldn't you want a spouse who was committed to care for you, no matter what?"

"Marriage is not about getting," John said. "It's about giving. And you might find that giving can be tremendously rewarding."

*****

"I must say that I was not greatly impressed by Skagway," Elroy said that evening at dinner. "A town of a few hundred people with a dozen bars."

"Again with that! You religious zealots hate fun," Dion said. "Bars are fun."

"Skagway was a pretty wild town in its heyday," John said. "There were even more bars and brothels then and very little law enforcement. The town was largely in the control of a nasty thug named Soapy Smith."

"I've heard of him," Elroy said.

"He and his gang ran a lot of the saloons and stores, and they would rob the gold seekers and murder them if they tried to fight back. And there was also a lot of robbery and violence besides what the gang was doing."

"Sounds like fun," Elroy said, glancing at Dion. "But that sort of thing happened in every gold rush town."

"Not every one," John said. "For an exception, you just have to look across that ridge of mountains that we could see in Skagway. On the Canadian side, the federal government sent in the Royal Canadian Mounted Police. They confiscated guns at the border—"

"Gun control?" Elroy asked.

"No general laws, just rules imposed by the police," John said. "There was still a lot of wild living in Dawson City, which was the center of the Yukon gold rush, but there was far less crime, and when crimes were committed, the perpetrators were often caught by the police. The police kept a tight lid on things."

"Dudley Doright," Autumn said. "How quaint. Do your police still ride horses and wear those floppy hats and red uniforms?"

"Only on ceremonial occasions," John said. "Most of them have traded in their horses for bicycles, and a few of them even have cars."

*****

"Are you enjoying the cruise?" Ruby asked later that evening.

"Very much," John answered. "Time off with you is always great, I'm enjoying seeing some new things, and even the table discussions are more interesting than I thought they might be."

"What do you think of our table companions?" Ruby asked.

"I was going to ask you the same question," John said. "For one thing, I don't think it's an accident that we keep running into Aiden and Alicia. They clearly want to talk to us about marriage."

"That's for sure. I also like Bob and Janet."

"Me too. But they don't talk a lot. I think there's something going on with those two, something that's bothering them maybe."

"Could be," Ruby agreed, "but they talk more than Celeste. I don't think I've heard her say anything other than what she wants to eat."

"Dion does the talking for both of them," John said, "and probably makes all the decisions too."

"Elroy and Letitia, on the other hand, do a lot of talking."

"Right. They are a lot of fun for sure," John said. "The Kinkaids talk, but they never seem to reveal very much. The rich have ways of maintaining walls to protect their privacy."

"And that's what the internet is for."

"What?" John asked.

"I looked them up. Thatcher works for Swiss Bordeleau, a big multinational. He's American and graduated from Harvard Business School. His expertise seems to be streamlining companies that Swiss Bordeleau takes over, cutting costs and making them more efficient."

"That's why he moves around. Autumn said he was just completing a contract assignment in British Columbia."

"Right," Ruby said. "Autumn is his second wife, by the way."

"What happened to his first wife?"

"It was a messy divorce. According to a tabloid story, she claimed he was, quote, a womanizer, but she couldn't prove it. He was able to produce evidence against her, and so she got very little in the settlement. I didn't find any information on what happened to her afterward."

Day Five

John and Ruby were just coming out of St Michael's Church in Sitka, Alaska, when they encountered Aiden and Alicia coming in.

"Hello, again," Ruby said.

"Oh, hi," Alicia said. "Um, can we talk to you some more?"

"Sure," Ruby said. "There are some benches over there under the trees. Let's sit there."

"We met on a cruise," Alicia said when they were sitting.

"Yes, you've already told us that," Ruby said.

"It was just a one-day excursion on the Fraser River," Aiden explained. "We work at the same IT company, and it was a reward for the employees for meeting the quarterly goals. It's a fairly large company, so we had never worked together, just seen each other a few times, but we started talking, and, well, it was magic. We got married six months later."

"The thing is, the magic's gone," Alicia said with a catch in her throat. "The thrill, the excitement, aren't there anymore. We've known it for some time. We're thinking about splitting up."

"So, I suggested we take this cruise as sort of a last attempt to save the relationship," Aiden said.

"And it's not working?" John suggested.

"No," Alicia said sadly.

"You thought boats had some magic power?" John asked.

"Well, we thought maybe if we got away together…but it's just like when we were back home," Alicia said.

"You listen to too many love songs. Love is not some overwhelming feeling that just carries you along," John said. "Love is a choice. Do you think Ruby gets up every morning, looks at me, and says, 'Wow, short, bald, and dumpy is the new tall, dark, and handsome'? No, she gets up every morning and chooses to keep loving me. And I get up every morning and choose to keep loving her—and with a lot more justification. I admire and respect her for a whole variety of reasons. She is worth loving."

"It's not that we don't have deep feelings for each other, we do, but feelings alone are a flimsy foundation to build a marriage on," Ruby added.

"Look, I still admire Aiden and all, but he doesn't make me happy anymore," Alicia said miserably.

"You expect Aiden to make you happy?" John asked. "That's a tremendous burden to place on any human being. No one has the power to make another person happy. I can try my best to make Ruby happy, and I do, but I can't do it all by myself."

"Before we got married, we realized that if we were not happy single, we would not be happy married," Ruby said. "It's the same thing now. If you're not happy married, you won't be happy single."

"Marriage can be a wonderful thing, but it can't be the only thing in your lives," John said. "You need a higher purpose."

Aiden looked up at St. Michael's. "You mean church?"

"Not church exactly," John said. "God. Church is just a place to find Him."

"Our parents used to take us to church when we were younger, and they insisted that we have a church wedding," Alicia said, "but we haven't been going for years."

"Maybe that's a place to start," John said.

*****

That evening had been labeled "a banquet," and guests had been instructed that the dress code was "formal." John wore his best three-piece dark suit, the one he reserved for "weddings, funerals, and other sad occasions." Ruby wore a dress she had bought on sale for a friend's wedding a couple of years ago. Dion wore the same powder blue silk suit, but added a scarlet bow tie for the occasion, while Celeste was wearing the same skimpy, red leather dress she had had on previously. The others were also wearing their best but modest clothes—except for the Kinkaids. Thatcher had a stylish tuxedo, and Autumn was arrayed in a stunning gold evening dress that glittered under the banquet room lights. Her necklace and other jewelry also shimmered, suggesting a price tag far beyond the cost of the cruise. But the conversation carried on as before.

"So, what do we all think of Sitka, the former capital of Russian Alaska?" Elroy asked.

"It certainly had a different flavor than Skagway or Ketchikan," John said.

"I was surprised that, according to the museum, the Russians treated the First Nations people worse than Americans did," Elroy said.

"Yes, interesting," John agreed.

"I would've thought you'd spend the whole day at that old church," Dion said, looking at John.

"Actually, maybe it's just my evangelical bias, but I found the church disappointing," John said. "They kept going on and on about their icons as if they were the most valuable things in the church."

"Yeah, the church gets rich, sucking up wealth from the poor," Dion said.

156

"So, John, in your opinion, what are the most valuable things in church?" Elroy asked.

"The people and the presence of God," John answered promptly. "Without those, church isn't worth anything, no matter how much gold and art are used to decorate it."

"What about that book that you zealots are always going on about?" Dion demanded.

"The Bible?" John said. "That's just a bit of paper and leather. What's really valuable is the message that's in the Bible."

"That it's okay for you to discriminate against other people, steal from the poor, and ruin everyone's fun with your narrow-minded morality?" Dion said.

"No, that God condemns all forms of injustice, but also that He loves us and offers forgiveness to us all," John said.

"I don't believe in your morality, and I don't need forgiveness," Dion said.

"Don't need forgiveness," Thatcher muttered.

There was a long silence.

"We also went shopping," Ruby said. "We bought one of those Russian dolls—you know, with the doll inside a doll inside a doll and so on."

"Dion bought two of them," Bob said, "but he bought two of the really big ones, a couple of feet high. We saw him leaving the store."

"Why can't you people mind your own business!" Dion exclaimed. "If you must know, of course, I bought two, one for me and one for Celeste."

Celeste suddenly pushed back from the table. "I need to use the washroom," she said. She stood and hurried from the room.

"I think you're just trying to compete with Autumn's jade bear," Janet suggested with a smile.

"I'm not going to apologize for having more money than you," Dion retorted. "If I want to buy something expensive, I will."

"Jade bear's better than a doll," Thatcher muttered.

There was a brief lull in the conversation.

Letitia stood up. "Power of suggestion," she said. "I need to use the washroom too." She also left the dining room.

"I'm afraid the conversation has become a little testy," Elroy said. "If you were my students, I would give you all a time-out. But that would be silly because we're all on vacation and we're already on a time-out."

"Good point," John said. "I find the philosophical idea behind those dolls quite intriguing."

"Good attempt at changing the subject, but they're dolls, John, not philosophical symbols," Elroy said.

"Sure, I know," John said. "They're fun. But think about it. There's the first doll that everybody sees, but inside there's another doll, and then another doll inside that, and so on. Remember we talked about everybody projecting a certain image but inside they might be quite different? Those dolls are like people—there are things hidden inside that we can't see from the outside."

"But the inside dolls look just like the outside dolls," Elroy said.

"Not exactly. The ones inside are smaller," John said.

"Like you said, you're smaller inside," Aiden said.

"No, I said I'm bigger in reality," John said.

"I don't believe it," Elroy said. "I think you're little all the way through."

Everyone laughed.

Elroy continued. "So, the analogy breaks down. But I do get your point. Some people are just like they appear in public, but other people are much different inside than the image they present to other people."

"Short people don't matter," Thatcher said quietly to no one in particular.

Letitia came back into the dining room and returned to the table.

"Where's Celeste?" Dion demanded.

"I don't know. I never saw her. We must have gone to different washrooms," Letitia said.

"Then where is she?" Dion repeated.

At that moment, Celeste came back in through the doors and returned to her place beside a scowling Dion.

*****

"Things got a little heated at dinner tonight," Ruby said later that night when they were back in their cabin.

"It wasn't just the food that was hot," John agreed.

"But I think it illustrated your point that people aren't always what they seem."

"Or maybe we were getting a glimpse of what was inside," John said.

"Maybe. Speaking of that, did Thatcher seem a little off tonight?"

"He was drinking quite a bit, I think. I wondered if he was drunk."

"Okay," Ruby said. "I also thought it was interesting that that was the first time that I've ever heard Celeste say anything, other than ordering her meal."

"She just said that she needed to use the washroom."

"Yes, but it was something."

"Maybe tomorrow she'll move on to discussing the weather."

*****

John looked at the digital clock. It read 2:51. Someone was knocking loudly on the door. John stumbled out of bed and went to the door. When he opened it, a steward was standing there and behind him Autumn Kinkaid in a stylish, white track suit.

"I am sorry to disturb you, sir," the steward said. "We were wondering if you had seen Mr. Kinkaid this evening or might know where he could be."

Behind the steward, Autumn pleaded, "He's missing. I don't know where he is."

John rubbed his eyes. "I'm sorry. I haven't seen him since dinner. We came back to our cabin right afterward and haven't left."

"Thank you, sir. I am sorry to have disturbed you," the steward said.

Crawling back into bed, John said, "I guess it pays to belong to the class that gets invited to the captain's table. If I went missing, I wonder if the stewards would look for me as promptly."

"Uhhmm," Ruby moaned.

"And I wonder if you would even notice."

Day Six

Prince Rupert is the most northern main port on Canada's west coast, a little south of the Alaskan Panhandle. When the *Arctic Adventure* pulled into the port early in the morning, Sergeant Wesson of the Royal Canadian Mounted Police was standing on the dock waiting, along with several other police officers from the Prince Rupert detachment. For the next couple of days, they would be on board. They were the closest police officers, indeed the only police officers, in the area. In their absence, Price Rupert would be policed by officers brought in from the towns of Terrace, Smithers, and Prince George to the east.

*****

It was only seven in the morning, and John and Ruby were beginning to stir when an announcement came over the speaker system: "This is your captain speaking. We are sorry to inform you that, due to some developments overnight, passengers and crew will not be allowed to leave the ship today and go ashore in Prince Rupert. Those of you who have booked shore excursions may go to the purser's office to arrange refunds. We are sorry to disappoint you, but this decision was made in cooperation with authorities in Prince Rupert and was deemed necessary. We ask that you all cooperate with the investigating authorities. We also want to assure you that there is no danger for any of you remaining on board, and onboard services will continue to be available. We hope to resume our journey later today as scheduled and will keep you informed."

"Oh, John, what could it be?" Ruby asked.

"I don't know. My best guess is that there has been an outbreak of some disease—Covid, norovirus, SARS, or flu or something."

"Then how could they say that we are in no danger?"

"Maybe they're just saying that to prevent panic."

"You mean we really could be in danger?"

*****

Half an hour later, there was a knock on their cabin door, and a steward was standing there when they opened it.

"John and Ruby Smyth?" he asked. "Would you please come with me?"

"Okay," John said. "What's this about? Do we need to bring anything?"

"There is no reason to worry," the steward said. "It would be helpful if you brought your identification papers, but other than that you don't need to bring anything. Everything will be explained to you shortly."

The steward led them to a small lounge on Deck D. Another steward checked their identification papers at the door. When they went inside, they saw Aiden and Alicia and Bob and Janet, as well as Roberto and some other crew members, sitting on chairs around tables. There were two doors on the back wall of the room.

"Do you know what is going on?" Aiden asked.

"My guess is that someone at our table is sick and they want to make sure it hasn't spread to the rest of us," John said.

"No talking please," the steward at the door said.

*****

A few minutes later, the door to an adjoining room opened. Another steward listened at the door, called out, "Roberto Diaz," and ushered Roberto inside the door.

A few more minutes passed, and another door, beside the first one, opened slightly. The steward listened at the door and then announced, "John Smyth."

John squeezed Ruby's hand, walked over, and went in through the door. The steward firmly shut it behind him. Inside was a large office area. A Royal Canadian Mounted Police officer was seated at a desk on the far side of the room. Another officer, who had apparently come to the door, was returning to another table off to one side; a laptop sat open on the table in front of her. John approached the desk, where there were two other chairs arranged facing the officer. The officer was looking at some papers on the desk in front of him.

"John Smyth," he said. "You are now one of my prime suspects."

"What?" John asked. He was in the process of sitting in one of the chairs when the officer raised his head. John froze. "Sergeant Wesson, what are you doing here? What's going on?"

"Good morning, Mr. Smyth," the sergeant said. "I'll ask the questions. What do you think is going on?"

"Well, I thought that there might be some sort of sickness on board, but unless you have switched careers and become a doctor, I don't think that's it."

"What I want to know is why you keep showing up in the middle of my investigations."

"If you're referring to that case a few years ago where you found dismembered bodies along the Yellowhead Highway, well, I just happened to be here in Prince Rupert for work. You know that."

"Yes, but that doesn't explain why you are here now."

"Ruby and I are on vacation, for our twenty-fifth anniversary."

"Congratulations, but it's still quite a coincidence."

"If you recall, I provided the key information to solve that other case."

"So, maybe you can provide some key information now," Wesson said. "What can you tell me about Thatcher Kinkaid?"

"Thatcher? I don't know much. He and his wife Autumn sit at our table at dinner. I had never heard of him before. They said he's an executive of some kind with a multinational company and he just finished an assignment or contract in British Columbia. Oh, they're from Arizona. Let me see. Ruby looked him up on the internet—"

"Why?"

"Why? I don't know. We didn't know much about him, they hadn't said much about themselves, and we were just curious."

"What did she find out?"

"His expertise seems to be streamlining companies that the multinational has taken over. And Autumn is his second wife. He's divorced from his first wife."

"What did you think of him personally?"

John scratched his bearded cheek. "I don't know. He didn't really reveal very much. You could tell he's used to money and power, and powerful people seem to know how to keep from revealing too much. Oh, and he seemed to be drinking fairly heavily last night. I think."

"Who did he interact with?"

"I only know him from the table. I think Roberto, our waiter, knew him from previous cruises. One night, he and Autumn were invited to eat at the captain's table." John shrugged.

"You're being extremely unhelpful," Wesson said.

"I thought policemen wanted witnesses to tell them everything and let the police decide what was relevant."

"You watch too much television."

"Why did you say I was a suspect?" John asked. "What am I suspected of? Did something happen to Thatcher? Did he fall overboard or something?"

"No."

"No, what?"

"No, he didn't fall overboard, and he wasn't pushed overboard. That's all you need to know. But let me know if you think of anything relevant," Wesson said. He pointed to another door at the side of the room. "You can get back to the corridor through that door."

Smyth had almost reached the door when he stopped and turned around. Just at that point, there was a knock on the other door, and a steward walked in.

"There's a couple out here who say they have something to say," the steward said.

A couple, who appeared to be in their fifties, came in behind the steward.

"Who are you?" Wesson demanded.

"Lawrence and Rebecca Broughton," the man said.

"Come and sit down and tell us what you have to say," Wesson instructed.

When they were seated, the man began. "We were seasick."

"And?" Wesson demanded.

"Last night, we were feeling pretty sick, so we took our buckets and went up on the top deck. There's more of a breeze up there, and the air seems fresher."

"And?"

"We were leaning on the rail looking down on the next deck, facing into the breeze, when we saw a man come out onto the deck pulling a big, red leather suitcase. He went over to the outside rail, looked around, and then he picked it up— it seemed very heavy—and he pushed it over into the water. We could hear the splash when it hit the water."

"And a few minutes later we heard another splash, but we didn't see anyone this time," Rebecca added.

"What did the man do after he pushed the suitcase into the water?" Wesson asked.

"He went straight back into the ship," Lawrence said.

"What time was this?"

"Right on twelve-thirty. I had just looked at my watch and suggested we should think about going back to our cabin," Lawrence said.

"Can you describe the man?" Wesson asked.

"He looked fairly tall and well built, he had curly, black hair down near his shoulders, and he was wearing a shiny light blue suit," Lawrence said.

"That sounds like Dion," John said.

"Mr. Smyth, why are you still here? I told you to leave," Wesson said.

"I'm sorry," John said. "I wanted to ask where I would find Ruby after her interview, but they walked in before I had a chance to say anything."

"You can wait in the corridor out there for Ruby," Wesson said. "But what did you mean it sounded like Dion? Who's Dion?"

"I don't know his last name, but he sits at our table too. He's with a woman named Celeste, but they aren't married."

"Never mind the morality lecture. I'm trying to solve a real crime," Wesson said. He looked down at his papers. "Ah, yes, he's on the list to be interviewed. You can leave now, Mr. Smyth. And I mean now."

*****

John went out into the corridor and found Ruby standing there.

"Ruby, how did you get out here?"

"I guess they have two people doing interviews. I got called into the other room right after you left. What do you think it's all about?"

"I think something must have happened to Thatcher Kinkaid," John replied. "They kept asking me what I knew about him. They said he didn't fall overboard or get pushed, but something must have happened."

"That's what they asked me about too," Ruby said, "but why were you in there longer than I was?"

"Well, the officer interrogating me was Sergeant Wesson, the man who led the investigation into those bodies they found on the highway outside Prince Rupert a few years ago."

"Oh, that's nice."

"It didn't feel very nice. He didn't seem glad to see me," John said. "And then, just as I was leaving, another couple came in and said they saw Dion throwing a suitcase over the rail into the ocean."

"That's weird."

As they were talking, they saw Roberto coming down the corridor.

"Roberto," John said. "Do you know what's going on? What's happened to Thatcher Kinkaid?"

Roberto looked uncomfortable. "I don't know if I'm supposed to say."

"But we know him," John said.

"It's very sad. Mr. Kinkaid was murdered last night."

"Murdered?" John asked.

"He was stabbed with an ice pick. It happened in the rear cafeteria late last night. He wasn't found until the staff came in around five this morning to get ready for breakfast. It's very sad."

"Thank you, Roberto," John said.

Roberto walked off down the corridor.

"If, for some reason, the police seem to be trying to keep everyone from knowing what happened," Ruby said, "how did Roberto know?"

John thought a moment. "The cafeteria staff found the body. Employees talk to each other."

"Maybe," Ruby said. "But didn't Roberto know Thatcher Kinkaid previously?"

*****

"Please go over and give your contact information to Constable Johnson," Wesson said to the Broughtons. He went to the door and said to the steward, "I want Dion Castelone in next."

The steward responded in a low voice, "We have brought in Castelone but we have not been able to find Celeste Burrowes, who is in the same cabin, and Castelone refuses to say where she is."

Wesson frowned. "Show Castelone in anyway."

The steward called out in a louder voice, "Dion Castelone."

As Dion was being shown into the room, Wesson walked across the lounge to the other door just as it opened. Wesson walked through, and the constable at the door shut the door behind him and followed him over to the desk. Another officer, wearing corporal's stripes, was sitting at the desk and looked up as Wesson approached.

"What's up?" he asked.

"Archbold, I want you and Constable Parker to join me for this next interview," Wesson said.

The two officers followed him into the lounge and through the other door into the first interview room. Wesson sat behind the desk while the other two officers remained standing just inside the door.

Wesson looked down at his papers and then looked up. "Dion Castelone?" he asked.

Dion shrugged.

"What do you do for a living, Mr. Castelone?"

"I'm a businessman."

"What kind of a businessman?"

Dion shrugged. I own a couple of stores."

"How many is a couple? Two?"

"Three."

"What are the stores called? What do you sell?"

"Grumpy Gizzard Weed and Vape."

Wesson nodded. "What can you tell me about Thatcher Kinkaid?"

"Not much," Dion said. "He's a rich and successful business executive, at least according to him."

"Richer and more successful than you?"

Dion shrugged.

"You sit at the same dining table as Kinkaid and his wife?" Wesson continued.

"So?"

"So, what do you think of him?"

Dion shrugged. "He acts like he is what he said he is, like he expects to always get his own way, I guess. He doesn't say much. He wasn't there one night."

"Where's Celeste Burrowes?" Wesson said suddenly.

Dion hesitated. "I'm not sure."

"Why not? You came on this trip together, and you're sharing a cabin, right?"

"We were," Dion said. "I don't know where she is now."

"When did you last see her?"

"Last night, around ten o'clock. I left the cabin to go to the casino for a bit, and when I came back, she was gone. I haven't seen her since."

"What time did you get back?"

"I'm not sure. About midnight."

"Did you report her missing? Aren't you worried about her?"

"No." Dion shrugged. "Celeste is a slut. She probably met some other man and went off with him."

"She's a slut. Is that why she's with you on this cruise?"

"Of course." Dion grinned.

Wesson nodded. "How well do you know her?"

"She hangs around some of the same bars I do. She seemed fun, so I invited her to come along."

"What do you know about her? Where does she come from?"

Dion shrugged. "I don't know. We don't talk much."

"Why did you throw a suitcase overboard last night?" Wesson demanded.

Dion looked shocked. "I didn't. Why would you think I would do something like that?"

"You were seen throwing a red leather suitcase over the railing at precisely twelve-thirty last night."

"Whoever says they saw me do that is wrong. I didn't do it. I was asleep in my cabin at twelve-thirty."

"What was in the suitcase?"

"Nothing. I don't know. I didn't do it. You've got the wrong man."

"You threw something else overboard a few minutes later. What was that?"

"I didn't do that either."

Wesson glared at Dion. "Stay here."

Wesson stood and went to the door, motioning to Archbold and Parker to follow him through the lounge and back to the other room.

Wesson spoke to Archbold. "I'll carry on with the interviews. I want you to get on to the captain and the coast guard and the FNCS. These ships all have GPS. Find out exactly where this ship was at twelve-thirty last night."

"That's a long shot, a very long shot," Archbold offered.

"Maybe, but we might get lucky. And authorize ten thousand dollars from the contingency fund on an emergency basis."

"That might help," Archbold agreed. "But that suitcase is probably at the bottom of the ocean. What do you think was in it?"

"Who knows? It could be his bloody clothes from when he killed Kinkaid. It could be Celeste Burrowes. It could be just clothes he didn't want anymore or something else. Celeste's body could have been the second splash a few minutes later. Or not. It's not even certain that Castelone threw a suitcase into the water."

"It's not?" Archbold asked.

"No. Two witnesses say they saw somebody throw a suitcase in the water, from behind, at a distance, in the dark. Another witness didn't see anything but heard the description and said it sounded like Castelone."

"That's decisive," Archbold said.

"I don't know whether we are dealing with one murder or two, but we need to investigate all possibilities. There are some other things I need you to do. Parker, bring Castelone to this room and keep him here."

"We're arresting him?" Parker asked.

"We're keeping him in custody for further questioning. Archbold, I also need you to secure Castelone's room, hopefully before the maids clean it today. Get a search warrant for it so we can look for evidence of where Celeste Burrowes might be. Then see if the ship has a more secure place to keep Castelone, even another vacant cabin would do. Then get the staff onshore to do a thorough background check on everyone at that table, and the waiter too. And tell the stewards I will need to reinterview everyone from that table and this time ask them about Castelone and Burrowes."

*****

"Again?" John Smyth asked when he was ushered into the interview room for a second time. "What do you want to know now?"

"What can you tell me about Dion Castelone?" Wesson said.

"I didn't know his last name, but I presume you mean the Dion who sits at our table in the dining room," John said. "I don't know much, only what he has said. He is opposed to traditional marriage. He seems only interested in having fun. He says he has no children that he knows of. He has a lot of gold jewelry, and he says he owns some retail stores. He's from Vancouver, I think."

"What about Celeste Burrowes?"

"Again, I didn't know her last name. I know even less since she never says anything. She seems totally under Dion's control. He doesn't treat her very well. I doubt if he has any intention of marrying her. I think he just invited her along for sex, and that seems to be all he thinks she's good for."

"You are very judgmental, Mr. Smyth."

"You asked me what I thought."

Wesson sighed. "When was the last time you saw Ms. Burrowes?"

"Last night at dinner. In fact, I think that's the only place I've ever seen her. I don't remember seeing her on deck or in any of the ports we visited. Of course, there are a lot of people, and it's a big ship, so that's not really surprising."

"Do you have any idea where she is now?"

"No. Why? Is she missing?"

170

"Not necessarily. We just haven't come across her. As you say, it's a big ship," Wesson said carefully. "Do you think Mr. Castelone is capable of harming Ms. Burrowes?"

John thought for a moment. "That's hard to say. I'm not sure if Dion is as hard and uncaring as he lets on. But, as you know, I have discovered that many people are capable of violence."

"How did the Kinkaids get on with Castelone and Ms. Burrowes? Was there any interaction between them?"

"Not that I saw, other than general conversation around the table," John said. "I wouldn't expect there would be. I doubt if they have much in common. Thatcher and Autumn are high society. They move in different circles from Dion and Celeste. And they're American, of course."

"But Mr. Kinkaid has apparently been working in British Columbia for the last few months."

John shrugged. "They might have run into each other before, but they didn't show any signs of recognizing each other when they first came to the table."

"Thank you, Mr. Smyth."

*****

The passengers milled about on deck as the *Arctic Adventure* pulled away from the dock in Prince Rupert to begin the final leg of the cruise.

"I feel a little like Moses gazing at the Promised Land from a mountaintop and not being allowed to enter," John said. "I was looking forward to seeing Paul Postos."

"And Sharon," Ruby said. "How long have they been pastoring the church here?"

"I'm not sure. Eight or ten years, I would think."

*****

"Is the ship really just going to go on to Vancouver on schedule?" Archbold asked. "Can't we hold it up until we finish our investigation?"

Wesson answered, "To disrupt the schedule would mean that the couple of thousand passengers currently on the ship might miss their connecting flights home. And there's another couple of thousand passengers waiting to get on, not to mention the thousands more on the next cruise and the one after that. And the towns in Alaska and British Columbia depend on the tourist trade. There are millions of dollars at stake. I asked, and it's out of the question. The government is not going to allow us to put so many people's lives on hold. We can't keep a couple of thousand people in custody indefinitely. We have to solve this murder before the ship docks in Vancouver sometime late tomorrow night."

*****

"Our numbers are greatly diminished," Elroy said that evening at the table.

"What exactly is going on?" Bob said. "The police asked a lot of questions but didn't tell us anything."

"Thatcher was found dead this morning," John answered. "He was stabbed last night in one of the cafeterias."

"Wow. I knew something had happened, but not that," Bob said. "Do they know who did it?"

"I don't think so," John said. "Roberto, do you know?"

Roberto stiffened. "As staff, we have been told not to discuss this. This is not a suitable topic for dinner conversation. Now, the appetizers for this evening are..."

*****

"Have you noticed that servants are often more insistent on observing proper protocol than the people they are supposed to be serving?" John asked when Roberto had gone to get the appetizers.

"You just think that because you are a peasant who doesn't know proper protocol," Elroy said. "I assure you that Thatcher and Autumn..." He stopped abruptly.

172

"Speaking of Autumn, does anyone know how she is doing?" Alicia asked.

There was a general shaking of heads.

"Sorry, no," John said.

"She must be devastated," Alicia said. "I don't think I could go to dinner if anything happened to Aiden."

"What about Dion and Celeste?" Janet asked. "Where are they?"

"The police don't seem to know where Celeste is, the last I heard," John said.

"They don't?" Letitia asked.

"No, and somebody saw Dion throw a suitcase overboard last night about twelve-thirty."

"Oh, no!" Janet said. "Did he do something to Celeste?"

John shrugged. "I think that's what the police are trying to find out."

"So that's why they asked us about Dion and Celeste," Bob said.

"It makes you think," Janet said. "Last night, there were six couples around this table, and now something has happened to two of them."

"It makes me grateful that we're still together and safe," Ruby said.

"It shows that anything could happen to any of us at any time," Aiden said thoughtfully.

Day Seven

"Okay, where are we?" Wesson said the next morning.

"We haven't found much," lead forensics investigator Dave Sutton said. "There were no fingerprints on the ice pick, the handle has a textured surface anyway. We are not hopeful about trace evidence. The problem is not that we can't find anything, but that there is just too much from too many people."

"And the pick itself?" Wesson asked.

"Standard for the ship. They are in every cafeteria and one in almost every cabin."

"Almost?" Wesson asked.

"Apparently, they are often pilfered by guests and aren't always replaced after each cruise," Sutton said.

"So, no way to tell where it came from?" Wesson asked.

"No," Sutton said. "From the blood spatter, we know there would have been considerable blood spray on the killer. We found some blood trace leading toward the door to the cafeteria but couldn't trace it farther. The staff vacuum the rugs in the corridors around the cafeteria every night."

"You searched the Kinkaids' cabin?" Wesson asked.

"Suite," Sutton said. "Three rooms. We found what you would expect, clothes and toiletries. There was a laptop there, and Thatcher had his cell phone with him. We are still looking at them, but there were no texts or calls last night, so if he agreed to meet someone, he must have arranged the meeting in person."

"You also searched Castelone's cabin, or did he have a suite too?" Wesson asked.

"Just a cabin in his case."

"I guess he is not as rich as Kinkaid," Wesson said.

"So, yes, we searched his cabin," Sutton said. "There was no blood evidence, so if he killed Kinkaid, he must have cleaned up somewhere else."

"What about Celeste Burrowes?" Wesson asked.

"We did not get there before the maid started cleaning," Sutton said. "There was still some evidence she had been there, hair and possibly fingerprints, but her clothes and luggage are missing."

"So, it's possible Castelone did throw her luggage overboard?" Archbold suggested.

"Possible, but she might also have taken her things with her when she left," Wesson said.

"Then, where is she?" Archbold asked. "There was that second splash."

"He could have killed her and thrown her overboard after her suitcase, but we can't prove that," Wesson said. "It was going to be hard enough solving one murder in two days. Solving two will be even harder."

"Unless they're linked," Archbold said.

"But are they linked? We don't know that either," Wesson said.

"Did you get anything from the interviews?" Archbold asked.

"Did you, from the ones you did?" Wesson responded.

"No."

"Neither did I," Wesson said. "There was the couple that reported seeing Castelone throw something overboard. The other witnesses claim not to have seen him that night, and none of them know much about him."

"What gets me," Archbold said, "is that there are no security cameras on this ship."

"People who take cruises want to get away. They are often well off and want privacy, and the cruise lines are happy to sell it to them," Wesson said.

"So, where does that leave us?" Archbold asked.

"We have a timeline for last night, such as it is," Wesson said. "Dinner ends around nine-fifteen, nine-thirty. Castelone goes to the casino around ten."

"We checked. The casino staff say he was there about that time but couldn't swear to the exact times," Archbold said.

"Castelone gets back to his cabin around twelve, he says, and finds Burrowes missing. According to his wife, Thatcher Kinkaid goes out to meet someone around ten-thirty. Mrs. Kinkaid is in the shower when he leaves and then goes to bed. She wakes up around two, sees her husband is not back, and asks the stewards to help her look for him. They search some of the common areas and wake up some of his table mates and some of the staff to ask if they have seen him. They give up after an hour or so and tell Mrs. Kinkaid to go back to her suite. Sutton, do we have a time of death for Kinkaid?"

"Our best guess is sometime between eleven and twelve-thirty," Sutton answered.

"Castelone is possibly seen throwing a suitcase overboard at twelve-thirty, and another splash is heard a few minutes later. Then there is nothing until the cafeteria workers find the body a little before five. Anything stand out to any of you?"

They looked at each other.

"Sounds like a whole lot of nothing," Archbold said.

"A whole lot of nothing is right," Wesson said. "And we're running out of time. Once the ship docks in Vancouver sometime overnight, we will have a couple of thousand suspects scattered all around the world and a crime scene trampled over by a few thousand more people. If we don't solve this in the next few hours, it's likely we won't ever solve it." He paused and then said abruptly, "I'm going on deck for a bit to clear my head."

*****

Bob Coates was standing by the railing watching the British Columbia forests slide away before him. John Smyth came up to stand beside him.

"How's it going?" John asked.

Bob nodded.

"Are you worried?" John asked.

"A little. I have skills and a good employment record. There are no guarantees, and it's not going to be easy to start over, but I expect I will find a job somewhere."

"There never are guarantees," John said. "And I will pray that you do find something."

Bob looked at John, assessing.

"But that's not what I meant," John went on. "I was wondering if you were worried about the police."

"Why would I be worried about the police?"

"Because Thatcher Kinkaid is the man who shut down your mill and cost you your job and your house."

"You figured that out?" Bob said.

"It wasn't hard, and easy to confirm with a little internet research."

"The thing is," Bob said. "Thatcher Kinkaid was brought in to shut down some mills, and he shut down some mills. If it wasn't him, it would have been somebody else. Thatcher Kinkaid is not responsible for mountain pine beetles, forest fires, and the environmental lobby that has decreased the supply of timber. Not much anybody can do about that."

"I hope Sergeant Wesson sees it that way when he finds out."

"He already knows. I told him when I was interviewed."

"That was smart."

Bob turned to John. "Do you think I killed Kinkaid?"

John hesitated a moment before responding.

*****

Wesson was leaning on the railing, morosely watching the scenery slide by and hoping for inspiration when he became aware of someone standing beside him.

"Is this your first cruise? How are you enjoying it?" John asked.

"That's not funny, Mr. Smyth," Wesson said.

"Maybe not, but you looked as if you could use some cheering up."

"Well, that's not going to do it. I need something more."

"The investigation's not going well?" John asked.

"You've probably heard by now that Thatcher Kinkaid has been murdered. Most murder investigations take weeks or months, sometimes years. We've only got two days to solve this one and maybe a missing persons case too. We're running out of time."

"Once the cruise is over, everyone involved will go home and be out of reach?" John said.

"Exactly."

"Then I'll pray that you solve it quickly."

Wesson turned and stared at John. "Pray? I told you last time that crimes are solved by skill, proper procedures, and hard work, not prayer."

"Paul Postos tells me that you have been attending church sometimes."

Wesson sighed. "You church people have too much time on your hands, always passing on useless gossip."

"It's not always useless," John said. "It's a way of keeping track of people and their needs. And, in my experience, sometimes it's even provided details that have helped to solve crimes."

"Not this time," Wesson said. "You got anything else?"

John was quiet for a moment. "Well, the Kinkaids are rich. That night was supposed to be a formal dinner. Thatcher wore a tuxedo that fit him like a glove, and Autumn wore a shiny gold evening gown. It probably cost more than we spent on the cruise. One day, in Ketchikan, I think, the Kinkaids bought a jade statue of a bear that was about a foot high. That must have cost a fortune. I think that might be why Dion bought two huge Russian dolls in Sitka. They were even bigger than the bear. Maybe Dion didn't want to be overshadowed by Thatcher and Autumn. I got the sense he's very competitive. It surprised me because he doesn't seem to be the type to buy dolls."

"Useless gossip." Wesson shook his head sadly. "Go away, Mr. Smyth."

*****

"Anything new?" Wesson asked when he returned to the temporary command center.

"We got a response from the FNCS," Archbold said. "And there's an Elroy Simmons here asking to talk to you."

*****

There had originally been twelve around the table, thirteen counting Roberto. Tonight, there were only six, John and Ruby Smyth, Bob and Janet Coates, and Aiden and Alicia King. Roberto was hovering, not sure whether to start taking appetizer orders.

Then, through the doors came Elroy and Letitia, followed by a third person not clearly visible behind Elroy's massive frame. Elroy and Letitia sat, and Celeste, appearing behind them, sat in Autumn's vacant seat.

Looking around at the startled faces, Elroy said, "What's the matter with yo all? Ain't yo never seen a black man afore?"

Before anyone else could say anything, another person entered the room and strode across to their table, sitting down in Dion's seat.

"Good evening. How are you all this evening?" Wesson said. "Order your appetizers, and then we can talk."

When the ordering business had been taken care of, all eyes turned toward Wesson.

"You should know that we have arrested Autumn Kinkaid for the murder of her husband Thatcher," Wesson said.

There were gasps all around the table.

Wesson continued. "We knew that whoever had stabbed Mr. Kinkaid would have been splattered with blood, but we found no blood on any of Mrs. Kinkaid's clothing. And then we discovered that her evening gown and a jade statue of a bear were missing. We think that the gown was thrown overboard and weighted down with the bear so it would sink. Looking closer, we found traces of blood on her shoes, which she didn't throw away, and some in the shower drain."

"Why would she kill her husband?" Alicia asked.

"Money, we suspect," Wesson said. "Mr. Kinkaid had a reputation for being unfaithful, and the marriage was not likely to last much longer. Mrs. Kinkaid knew that when Mr. Kinkaid divorced his first wife, she got almost nothing in the settlement. She didn't want that to happen to her. If he was dead, she would get everything."

"And what about...?" Elroy said.

Wesson nodded. "The breaking point, we think, came when...well, that last night, Mr. Kinkaid made an arrangement with Mr. Castelone to—for want of a better word—'rent' Ms. Burrowes for the evening."

Cesleste looked down. "I was scared," she said. "I was afraid he would beat me if I didn't go along with it."

"Celeste told me about it when we both went out to the washroom that night at dinner, and we agreed to hide her in our cabin," Letitia said.

"Which you didn't tell the police," Wesson said sharply. "That was not helpful."

"But we didn't know you were even looking for her," Elroy protested. "We thought you were focused on the murder."

"What about the suitcase?" John asked.

"Oh, yes," Wesson said. "Mr. Castelone seems to have a vindictive streak. When he found out that Ms. Burrowes did not go along with his arrangement and had gone off somewhere else, he packed all her belongings into her suitcase and threw it into the ocean."

There were more startled gasps around the table. The appetizers had arrived, but no one was eating. They sat cooling on the table. Roberto was hovering in the background.

"You will be happy to learn, Ms. Burrowes," Wesson said, "that we have recovered your suitcase, and it will be flown to Vancouver for you."

"How?" Celeste said.

"Ship movements nowadays are tracked by GPS and satellite. Someone had seen Mr. Castelone throw the suitcase overboard, so we knew the time. From that, we were able to determine where to look. We asked the FNCS—the First Nations Conservation Societies—to be on the lookout for it. The government has made an arrangement with the local First Nations to monitor the coast for environmental and other issues. They are routinely on the water anyway. And we offered a small reward."

"I'm surprised it didn't sink," Ruby said.

"It probably would have eventually," Wesson said, "but fortunately the wake of the ship pushed it onto the rocks of a small island."

"Sounds like an answer to prayer to me," John said quietly.

Wesson ignored him.

"What did Dion say about the suitcase?" Ruby asked.

"He denied it, of course," Wesson said. "And when he found out what had happened to Mr. Kinkaid, he didn't know if Ms. Burrowes could have been involved, and he didn't want us knowing about his arrangement, so he just shut up and refused to talk."

"Where is he now? Is Celeste still in danger?" Alicia asked.

"No, Ms. Burrowes is safe," Wesson answered. "Mr. Castelone is also in custody."

"For the way he treated Celeste?" Alicia asked.

"No. It turns out that when he was in Sitka, Mr. Castelone purchased a couple of Russian dolls, much larger than the usual ones."

"Useless gossip," John muttered.

"Be quiet, Mr. Smyth," Wesson said. "We became curious and checked out the dolls. The outer dolls were made of wood as usual, but the smallest doll inside was glued shut. Inside it, we discovered several pounds of cocaine and fentanyl."

One Year Later

"We got some important mail today," Ruby said when John came home.

"What?" John asked.

"A letter from Aiden and Alicia, with a picture of their new baby." Ruby handed him the photo.

"Wonderful! She's cute."

"Yes. She obviously gets her looks from her mother and not her father."

www.ingramcontent.com/pod-product-compliance
Lightning Source LLC
Chambersburg PA
CBHW060420310726
48976CB00003B/1132